2/02

D0458539

I Cannot
Tell a Lie,
Exactly

I Cannot Tell a Lie, Exactly

And Other Stories

Mary Ladd Gavell

RANDOM HOUSE

NEW YORK

"The Rotifer" was originally published in *Psychiatry* magazine in 1967.

Library of Congress Cataloging-in-Publication Data
Gavell, Mary Ladd.
    I cannot tell a lie, exactly : and other stories / Mary Ladd Gavell.— 1st ed.
        p.   cm.
    ISBN 0-375-50612-8 (acid-free paper)
    1. United States—Social life and customs—20th century—Fiction.   I. Title.
PS3557.A9546 R67 2001
813'.54—dc21

                                                            2001019105

Random House website address: www.atrandom.com

Printed in the United States of America on acid-free paper

9   8   7   6   5   4   3   2
First Edition
Book design by Caroline Cunningham

To the sons of Mary Ladd Gavell, Stefan Michael Gavell and Anthony Christopher Gavell, and to her granddaughters, Sophie Kim Gavell and Stephanie Gina Gavell

Contents

Introduction

by Kaye Gibbons

One of the chief reasons that the stories contained within these covers are so magnificent is, simply put, because they belong to the ageless, classic grand era of the modern American short story. Readers need Mary Ladd Gavell's work to be added to the literary canon. Writers need her as well. We all need reminding that the principal aims of literature are to create joy, to delight, and to instruct, not in the sense of changing our politics but in leading us to a full, vibrant, and authentic sense of purpose, both tasks mandated by Horace and, woefully, almost sequentially buried, over the last twenty years, with the old masters. Elizabeth Spencer,

Grace Paley, and Eudora Welty are our living wonders, proof that a story about family, need, hope, and grace can be told thoroughly without hubris, with humor and candor, with hope fixated on the person turning each page and having a wonderful time. Maybe this is because writers of their generation came of age during the Depression and developed a respect for life commensurate with the tragedy of it all; maybe it is because of their strong, intact family and community loyalties; maybe it is because there used to be, as Flannery O'Connor said, a "habit of being" in the way one went about an existence that was more predictable than the jangled-up one today. Maybe it is because the greatest short stories were written before television vacuumed magazine and literary-journal readers away from newsstands. Maybe all these factors contribute to the quiet certainty of Gavell's tales, the calm, patient exactitude that draws her into such grand company. There is in her narratives the elegance of Katherine Anne Porter, a fellow Texan, a mingling of loneliness and regret not seen outside of Fitzgerald's "Babylon Revisited," and testaments to mothers and children, as well as one's opinion of the other, always handled with care and an awe characteristic of Peter Taylor. Gavell can write about anybody, anything, any place—town, country, smart, stupid, gullible, wise, heartbroken, happy, rough, rich. It is amazing. Her range is formidable.

The first trait evident in the collection is a self-assured yet reticent voice that will not admit entrance to arrogance, a sense of a cleverly manipulative author generating and controlling the narrative, calling attention to herself at every turn. Gavell calls attention, instead, to characters we want to know, thus to language we want to hear them speak, and then to plot, which is sometimes just a simple arrangement of extraordinary events that rattle an otherwise ordinary day: A plasterer gets caught up in a bargain that changes his life and allows him to come home once in a while with liquor on his breath. A student becomes focused on and escapes into another life, and this peering in becomes the metaphor for her scientific scrutiny.

In 1963, Frank O'Connor wrote that the short story was the national art form, and indeed it was. Not only did the truncated length of the short story suit our brief history, our lack of hundreds of pages of socialized angst that could be poured into a *War and Peace,* but the form had been highly marketable since the rise of popular magazines at the close of the Civil War. Also, it allowed a single writer the freedom to range at will among many voices without committing for great lengths of time to a novel. Gavell was hitting the mark as well as her contemporaries, such as Jean Stafford and Grace Paley, when O'Connor made this observation on the wealth of American storytelling. (She must have had stores of willpower, as well as confidence in her own intelligence and in the power and precision of her creativity, to write story after story without the steady encouragement that public acceptance can offer.)

Any writer who can successfully hide out in a short story is someone who has probably grown up listening to the particular rhythms, cadences, and turns of phrase of a region, and it was perhaps first in the stories of Mark Twain that a truly American voice was heard in this abbreviated form. There was Poe, but with him there was the unrelenting reminder of the ingenious teller behind the tale. Gavell in "Sober, Exper., Work Guar." withdraws and lets the story unwind in spirited colloquial language, with the resident craftsman/narrator primed always to offer the reader any advantage of irony, comedy, misunderstanding, and class intrigue he can, and we are thoroughly grateful. In "Yankee Traders" Gavell also works, as Twain did, on the nuances, subtle or not, of one collection of people staged in mental combat against another.

Reading these stories is a reminder of what is so very fine about our literature, and what needs to be preserved, in the main: our regional language against homogenization. Mrs. Gavell studied early Texas English, and her love of turns of phrase, her appreciation for the language of childhood memory, is evident in stories in which Corpus Christi represents unbridled sophistication and daily life on the farm with broods of children and hogs and cows is as fierce as it is in Katherine Anne Porter's "He." For some of Gavell's characters, memory is as vast and deep, and at times as confusing and intolerable, as it is in Porter's master-piece, "Pale Horse, Pale Rider." Faulkner's "That Evening Sun" is perhaps the most intensely regional short story of the century, in speech, dialect, and tone, but it is lifted out of the local, as are Gavell's "The Cotton Field," "The School Bus," and others, by the over-whelming, universally shared emotions of love, fear, re-gret, and transgression. And if those were not enough, mix in the memories through which some of her stories are told, particularly those of women who live long enough to despise loneliness and disdain the apparent ease with which others are getting by in life.

Gavell is a master at painting quiet regret and sti-fled sorrow, sometimes expressing thought and feel-ing with the spartan signatures of Hemingway's *In Our Time,* at other times compounding descriptions to achieve a density that would be ruined by just one more word. There is a certain Gavell story in which a woman is dying and knows the truth, when around her swirls a lie she is powerless to correct. So she must let it be, let everything be forever as it is at that moment, even though she needs desperately to explain herself. The publication of these stories is something of a re-minder of that woman's desire to tell what is on her mind now, what she is aching to say. Within these pages, Gavell writes of several splendid mothers who, by their labor, devotion, sacrifice, and small but loving acts—shaping a George Washington wig on a moment's notice, for instance—plainly want their children to be proud of them. As a writer and as a mother, I know that all those who have loved Mary Ladd Gavell will be enormously proud of her accomplishments here. She takes her stand among the best of our time.

A Memory of

My Mother

by Anthony C. Gavell

Mary Ladd Gavell's writing reflects her Texas origins. She grew up in the tiny farming community of Driscoll in a Texas just a generation removed from the frontier era. Her parents were farmers and schoolteachers who placed a high value on education. Her own mother was a strong and independent woman who held a master's degree in English, an unusual accomplishment for a woman of that time and place. My mother came of age during the Great Depression, and although her family was in very modest circumstances they provided a supportive atmosphere that encouraged her to set no limits on what she could be. After completing her education with a master's degree in linguistics she had the drive and ambition to leave Texas and eventually work for an international organization in Washington, D.C., before becoming an editor.

She had a rare gift for friendship and laughter. Her sense of humor, often of the self-deprecating variety, and her unique viewpoint were a delight to her friends. She was a wonderful conversationalist and raconteur. She was interested in people and tended to see the best in them. Her writing sprang from her interest in human nature and daily life's little dramas. She could write or tell a story about some ordinary event like buying a new hat and turn it into an epic adventure with all kinds of humorous twists and turns. Yet she could also touch on deeper themes, as she does in many of her short stories. A down-to-earth and sometimes feisty lady, she also loved poking gentle fun at pomposity and pretense.

Mary Ladd Gavell was that rare person: both an artist and a woman of great common sense and practicality; her artistic bent extended to drawing, music, and sculpture. She was also a prolific writer of letters to family and friends. Her family is fortunate to have a collection of hundreds of her letters written over the course of her life. They are full of wit and warmth and her genius for finding the wonder in everyday life. Like all her writing, they reflect her profound human sympathy and gentle humor. The letters also illustrate how effortlessly she wrote such clear, polished prose. Each sentence, even entire paragraphs, seemed to come out of her head perfectly formed; an editor would have found little to change in even her most casual writings. My mother also loved to read; among her favorite authors were Jane Austen and Mark Twain, whose influence I believe is reflected in her work.

She was something of an early feminist. In the stifling, conformist climate of the postwar years, she knew she wanted more out of life than marriage and raising children. She saw no reason why someone less capable than herself should enjoy advantages solely by virtue of being born male. She was never one to defer automatically to male authority, but was a woman of such natural tact and charm she never asserted herself in an abrasive way.

As one of her two children, I knew her mainly as a parent whom I lost all too soon. As a mother, she was indulgent and kindhearted. She had great respect for her children's individuality and always encouraged us to find and develop our particular talents and abilities. She did not talk down to us, and she treated us as much like adults as our age allowed. She preferred to appeal to our reason rather than force us to do things. She obviously enjoyed her children very much, and much of what we said and did found its way into her letters and stories. (I am the basis for Jimmie in the story "I Cannot Tell a Lie, Exactly.") One day when I was in first grade I burst into tears and refused to go to school. I said I was "too tired to do all that writing." She allowed me to stay home. As she wrote to a friend, "Older people than he have taken a day off for worse reasons, so he's spending a nice day at home regressing and watching *Captain Kangaroo*."

I Cannot Tell a Lie, Exactly

The Swing

As she grew old, she began to dream again. She had not dreamed much in her middle years; or, if she had, the busyness of her days, converging on her the moment she awoke, had pushed her dreams right out of her head, and any fragments that remained were as busy and prosaic as the day itself. She had only the one son, James, but she had also mothered her younger sister after their parents died, and she had done all of the office work during the years when her husband's small engineering firm was getting on its feet. And Julius's health had not been too good, even then; it was she who had mowed the lawn and had helped Jamie to learn to ride his bicycle and pitched balls to him in the backyard until he learned to hit them.

But she was dreaming again now, as she had when she was a child. Oh, not the lovely, foolish dreams of finding oneself alone in a candy store, or the horrible dreams of being pursued through endless corridors without doors by nameless terrors. But as her days grew in quietness and solitude—for James was grown and gone, and Julius was drawing in upon himself, becoming every day more small and chill and dim—color and life and drama were returning to her dreams.

But on that first night when she heard the creak of the swing, she did not think that she was dreaming at all. She had been lying in bed quite awake, she thought, in the little room that used to be Jamie's—for nowadays her reading in bed, and afterward her tossing and turning, disturbed Julius. The swing was not an ordinary one. Julius had put it up, in one of the few flashes of poetry in all his worrisome, hardworking life, when Jamie was only a baby and nowhere near old enough to swing in it. The ladder Julius had was not tall enough, and he had to buy a new one, for the tree was tremendous and the branch on which he proposed to hang the swing arched a full forty feet from the ground, and much thought and consideration and care were given to the chain, and the hooks, and the seat. The swing was suspended from so high, and its arc was so wide, that riding in it was like sailing through the air with the leisurely swoop of a wheeling bird. One seemed to travel from one horizon to the other. And how proud Julius had been of it when Jamie was old enough to swing in it, and the neighborhood children had stood around to admire and be given a turn, for there was no other swing like it.

The swing was hardly ever used now; it was only a treat, once in a while, for a visiting child, and occasionally when she was outside working in her flower border she would sit and rest in it for a moment or two, idling, pushing herself a little with a toe. But the rhythmic creak of the chains was so familiar that she could not mistake it, she thought. Could the wind be strong enough to move it, if it came from the right angle? She finally gave up thinking about it and went to sleep.

Nor did she think of it the next day, for they were due for Sunday dinner at James's house. He lived in a suburb on the opposite side of the city—just the right distance away, she often thought, far enough so that aging parents could not meddle and embarrass and interfere, but near enough so that she could see him fairly often. She loved him with all her heart, her dear, her only son. She was enormously proud of him, too; he was a highly paid mathematician in a research foundation, an expert in a field so esoteric that she had given up trying to grasp its point. But secretly she took some credit, for it was she—who had kept the engineering firm's books balanced and done the income tax—who had played little mathematical games with him before he had ever gone to school and had sat cross-legged with him on the floor tossing coins to test the law of probability. Oh, they had had fun together in all sorts of ways; they had done crossword puzzles together, and studied the stars together, and read books together that were over his head and sometimes over hers too. And he had turned out well; he was a scholar, and a success, and a worthy citizen, and he had a pretty wife, a charming home, and two handsome children. She could not have asked for more. He was the light and the warmth of her life, and her heart beat fast on the way to his house.

She drove. She had always enjoyed driving, and nowadays Julius, who used to insist on doing it himself, let her do it without a word. They drove in silence mostly, but her heart was as light as the wind that blew on her face, and she hummed under her breath, for she was on her way to see James. Julius said querulously, "I could have told you you'd get into a lot of traffic this way and you'd do better to go by the river road, but I knew you wouldn't listen," but she was so happy that she forbore to mention that whenever she took the river road he remarked how much longer it was, and only answered, "I expect you're quite right, Julius. We'll come back that way."

They did go home by the river road, and it seemed very long; she was a little depressed, as she often was when she returned from James's house. "I love him with all my heart"—the words walked unbidden into her mind—"but I wish that when I ask him how he is he wouldn't tell me that there is every likelihood that the Basic Research Division will be merged with the Statistics Division." He had kissed her on the cheek, and Anne, his wife, had kissed her on the cheek, and the two children had kissed her on the cheek, and he had slipped a footstool under her feet and had seated his father away from drafts, and they had had a fire in the magnificent stone fireplace the architect had dreamed up and the builder added to the cost, and Anne had served them an excellent dinner, and the children had, on request, told her of suitable A's in English and Boy Scout merit badges. They had asked her how she had been, and she told them, in a burst of confidence, that she had had the ancient piano tuned and had been practicing an hour a day. They looked puzzled. "What are you planning to do with it, Mother?" Anne asked. "Oh, well nothing, really," she said, embarrassed. She said later on that she had been reading books on China for she was so terribly ignorant about it, and they asked politely how her eyes were holding up, and when she said that she was sick of phlox and was going to dig it all up and try iris, James said mildly, "You really shouldn't do all that heavy gardening anymore, Mother." They were loving, they were devoted, and it was the most pleasant of ordinary family Sunday afternoons. James told her that he had another salary increase, and that the paper he had delivered before the Mathematical Research Institute had been, he felt he could say without exaggeration, most well received, and that they were getting a new station wagon. But what, she wondered, did he feel, what did he love and hate, and what upset him or made him happy, and what did he look forward to? Nonsense, she thought, I can't expect him to tell me his secret thoughts. People can't, once they're grown, to their parents. But the terrible fear rose in her that these *were* his secret thoughts, and that was all there was.

That night she heard the swing again, the gentle, regular creak of the chains. What *can* be making that noise, she wondered, for it was a still night, with surely not enough wind to stir the swing. She asked Julius the next day if he ever heard a creaking sound at night, a sound like the swing used to make. Julius peered out from his afghan and said deafly, "Hah?" and she answered irritably, "Oh, never mind." The afghan maddened her. He was always chilly nowadays, and she had knitted the afghan for him for Christmas, working on it in snatches when he was out from under foot for a bit, with a vision of its warming his knees as they sat together in the evenings, companionably watching television, or reading, or chatting. But he sat less and less with her in the evenings; he went to bed very early nowadays, and he had taken to wearing the afghan daytimes around his shoulders like a shawl. She was sorry immediately for her irritation, and she tried to be very thoughtful of him the rest of the day. But he didn't seem to notice; he noticed so little now.

Other things maddened her too. She decided that she should get out more and, heartlessly abandoning Julius, she made a luncheon date with Jessie Carling, who had once been a girl as gay and scatterbrained as a kitten. Jessie spent the entire lunch discussing her digestion and the problem of making the plaids match across the front in a housecoat she was making for herself. A couple of days later, she paid a call on Joyce Simmons, who had trouble with her back and didn't get out much, and Joyce told her in minute detail about her son, dwelling, in full circumstantial detail, on the virtues of him, his wife, and his children. She held her tongue, though it was hard. My trouble, she thought wryly, is that I think my son is so really superior that a kind of noblesse oblige forces me not to mention it.

The next time she heard it was several nights later. She sat up in bed and, half aloud, said, "I'm not dreaming, and it *certainly* is the swing!" She threw on her robe and her slippers and went downstairs, feeling her way in the dark carefully, for though sounds seemed not to reach Julius, lights did wake him. Softly she unlocked the back door and, stepping out into the moonlight, picked her way through the wet grass, holding her nightgown up a little. When she got beyond the thick grove of trees and in sight of the big oak, she saw it, swooping powerfully through the air in its wide arc, and the shock it gave her told her that she had not really believed it. There was a child in the swing, and she paused with a terrible fear clutching at her. Could it be a sleepwalking child from somewhere in the neighborhood? And would it be dangerous to call out to the child, or would it be better to go up and put out a hand to catch the swing gently and stop it? She walked nearer softly and slowly, afraid to startle the child, her heart beating with panicky speed. It seemed to be a little boy and, she noticed, he was dressed in ordinary clothes, not pajamas, as a sleepwalker might be. Nearer she came, still undecided what she should do, shaking with fear and strangeness.

She saw then that it was James. "Jamie?" she cried out questioningly, and immediately shrank back, feeling that she must be making some kind of terrible mistake. But he looked and saw her, and, bright in the moonlight, his face lit up, as it had used to do when he saw her, and he answered gaily, "Mommy!"

She ran to him and stopped the swing—he had slowed down when he saw her—and knelt on the mossy ground and put her arms around him and he put his arms around her and squeezed tight. "I'm so glad to see you!" she cried. "It's been such a long time since I've seen you!"

"I'm glad to see you too," he cried, grinning, and kissed her teasingly behind the ear, for he knew it gave her goose bumps. "You know," he said, "I like this swing. I like to swing better than anything, and I can pretend I'm a pilot flying an airplane, and sometimes I go *r-r-r-r* and that's the engine."

"Well," she said, "it is sort of like flying. Like an airplane, or maybe like a bird. Do you remember, Jamie, when you used to want to be a bird and would wave your arms and try to fly?"

"That was when I was a real little kid," he said scornfully.

She suddenly realized that she didn't know how old he was. One tooth was out in front; could that have been when he was six? Or seven? Surely not five? One forgot so much. She couldn't very well ask him; he would think that very odd, for a mother, of all people, should know. She noticed, then, his red checked jacket hanging on the nail on the tree; Julius had given him that jacket for his sixth birthday, she remembered now; he had loved it and had insisted on carrying it with him all the time, even when it was too warm to wear it, and

Julius had driven a little nail in the oak tree for him to hang it on while he swung; the nail was still there, old and rusty.

"Mommy, how high does an airplane fly?" he asked.

"Oh, I don't know," she said, "two thousand feet, maybe."

"How much is a foot?"

"Oh, about as long as Daddy's foot—I guess that's why they call it that."

"Have people always been the same size?"

"Well, not exactly. They say people are getting a little bigger, and that most people are a little bigger than their great-granddaddies were."

"Well [she saw the trap too late], then if feet used not to be as big, why did they call it a foot?"

"I don't know. Maybe that isn't why they call it a foot. We should look it up in the dictionary."

"Does a dictionary tell you *everything*?"

"Not everything. Just about words and what they mean and how they started to mean that."

"But if there's a word for everything, and if a dictionary tells you about every word, then how can it help but tell you about everything?"

"Well," she said, "you've got a good point there. I'll have to think that one over."

Another time he would ask, "Why is it, if the world is turning round all the time, we don't fall off?"

"Gravity. You know what a magnet is. The earth is just like a big magnet."

"But where *is* the gravity? If you pick up a handful of dirt, it doesn't have any gravity."

"Well, I don't know. The center of the earth, I guess. Well, I don't really know," she said.

She felt as if the wheels of her mind, rusty from disuse, were beginning to turn again, as if she had not engaged in a real conversation, or thought about anything real, in so long that she was like a swimmer out of practice.

They talked for an hour, and then he said he had to go, with the conscientious keeping track of time he had used to show when it was time to go to school.

"See you later, alligator," he said, and the answer sprang easily to her lips: "After a while, crocodile."

He came every night or two after that, and she lay in bed in happy anticipation, listening for the creak of the swing. She did not go out in her robe again; she hastily dressed herself properly, and put on her shoes, for she had always felt that a mother should look tidy and proper. There by the swing they sat, and they talked about the stars and where the Big Dipper was, and about what you do about a boy who is sort of mean to you at school *all* the time, not just now and then, the way most children are to each other, only they don't especially mean it, and about what you should say in Sunday school when they say the world was made in six days but your mother has explained it differently, and about why the days get shorter in winter and longer in summer.

She bloomed; she sang around the house until even Julius noticed it, and said, disapprovingly, "You seem to be awfully frisky lately." And when Anne phoned apologetically to say that they would have to call off Sunday dinner because James had to attend a committee meeting, she was not only perfectly understanding—as she always tried to be in such instances—but she put down the phone with an utterly light heart, and took up her song where she had left it off.

Then one night, after they had talked for an hour, Jamie said, "I have to go now, and I don't think I can come again, Mommy."

"Okay," she said, and whatever reserve had supplied the cheerful matter-of-factness with which she had once taken him to the hospital to have his appendix out, when he was four, came to her aid and saw to it that there was not a tremor in her voice or a tear in her eye. She kissed him, and then she sat and watched as he walked down the little back lane that had taken him to school, and off to college, and off to a job, and finally off to be married—and he turned, at the bend in the road, and waved to her, as he always used to do.

When he was out of sight, she sat on the soft mossy ground and rested her arms in the swing and buried her face in them and wept. How long she had sat there, she did not know, when a sound made her look up. It was Julius, standing there, frail and stooped, in the moonlight, in his nightshirt with the everlasting afghan hung around his thin old shoulders. She hastily tried to rearrange her attitude, to somehow make it look as if she was doing something quite reasonable, sitting there on the ground with her head pillowed on the swing in the middle of the night. Julius had always felt she was a little foolish and needed a good deal of admonishing, and now he would think she was quite out of her mind and talk very sharply to her.

But his cracked old voice spoke mildly. "He went off and left his jacket," he said.

She looked, and there was the little red jacket hanging on the nail.

The Rotifer

I

Though I sit hunched studiously over my microscope, I am gazing dreamily past it and out the open window, at the lazy afternoon campus. But the lab instructor, a graduate student who stutters a little and dreams of the day when he will be an assistant professor, comes hovering down the row of tables, and I return to my microscope. I do not plan to become a biologist. Two sciences are Required, and I regard with detachment the sophomores' frogs' legs and sheep's livers, each with a name tag attached, which float in the barrel of formaldehyde in the corner. It gives off a technical, advanced, arcane smell, but it does not stir me. Next year I shall be off to another lab and another science and shall putter about with bunsen burners or magnetic fields.

It is late in the fall, although it is still warm here in Texas, and the faint sounds of football practice drift in through the open window. We forty freshmen in this room have, since our arrival at the state university from the sleepy cactusy towns and the raw cities and the piney woods and the plains, been learning of the protozoa, the one-celled creatures who simply divide when they want to become two, and are not always sure whether they are plants or animals. The lab instructor has hovered over us yearningly, wanting us to get a *good* view of the amoeba, to really *appreciate* the spyrogyra.

But today, as he gives each of us a glass slide with a drop of pond water on it, he tells us that we are leaving the protozoa and beginning the long evolutionary climb. Today we shall see the rotifers, who belong to the metazoa. We too, at the other end of the microscope, are metazoa; the rotifer, like us, has a brain, a nervous system, and a stomach.

I am fairly good, by this time, at adjusting my microscope. I know that those long, waving fronds are reflections of my own eyelashes, and I recognize algae when I see it, greenish leafy stuff rather like the broccoli on a dormitory dinner plate. Soon I find the rotifers—furiously alive, almost transparent little animals, churning powerfully along in their native ocean.

Watching, I am a witness to a crisis in the life of a rotifer. He is entangled in a snarl of algae, and he can't get loose. His transparent little body chugs this way and that, but the fence of algae seems impenetrable. He turns, wriggles, oscillates, but he is caught. *Rest a moment,* I whisper to him, *lie still and catch your breath and then give a good heave to the left.* But he is in a wild panic, beyond any reasonable course of action. It seems to me that his movements are slowing down, as if he is becoming exhausted.

Maybe I can help him. Perhaps I can put my finger on the edge of the glass slide and tip it ever so slightly, tilt it just enough so that the water will wash him over the barrier. Cautiously, gently, I touch the slide.

But the result is a violent revolution in the whole rotifer universe! My rotifer and his algae prison wash recklessly out of sight, and whole other worlds of rotifers and algae and amoebae and miscellaneous creatures of the deep reel by, spinning on the waves of a cataclysm. My rotifer is gone, lost to me. Huge and clumsy, more gargantuan than any Gulliver, I am separated from him forever by my monstrous size, and there is no way I can get through from my dimension to his.

The bell rings; lab is over. I take my slide out from under my microscope; there on it is the merest drop of water, and I look at it uncertainly. I start to wipe it off, to put the slide away, but I hesitate and look at it again. The lab instructor, seeing me still standing there, hurries over. "Did you get a *good* conception of the ciliary movement?" he asks me anxiously.

"I guess so," I answer, and I polish the slide until it is dry and shiny and put it away.

II

Like that earnest young man, the lab instructor, I became, for a little while a few years later, an intellectual sharecropper, as we called young graduate students who had various ill-defined and ill-paid functions around the university. During this period I was for some reason handed the job of going through the papers of the Benton family, which a descendant, looking for something suitable to do with them, had turned over to the university. The Bentons had been a moderately prominent family who had moved from the East to Tennessee in the 1790s, and then, thirty or so years later, to the Southwest. They were notable for having been respectable, prosperous, God-fearing, and right-doing lawyers and landowners, and they were also notable for having saved most of the papers that came into their hands.

All these qualities had culminated in Josiah Benton, who had been State Treasurer in the 1840s and had saved every paper he got his hands on.

So for weeks and weeks, I sat in a corner of the archives library and turned through fragile and yellowed papers, making out the dim and faded handwriting of Benton love letters, lists of Benton expenditures for curtain material and camisoles, reports and complaints to various Bentons from their tenants, letters to traveling Benton husbands from Benton wives, bills of sale for Benton slaves, political gossip from Benton cronies and domestic gossip from Benton relatives, diaries begun and never finished, and a few state papers filched by Josiah, like many another bureaucrat after him, from the official files.

It was impossible not to become interested in the Bentons. I sat down with those boxes of ancient gossip and circumstance more eagerly than I asked a friend, what's new? Lydia May Benton feuded with her sister-in-law Sally, and the mysterious trouble about Jonathan Benton, it turned out, was that he *drank*. Aunt Millie Benton's letters to her traveling husband began and ended with protestations of devotion and obedience, but in between she told him what to do and when to do it. But if Josiah's wife, Lizzie, had ever had an opinion, it went unrecorded; when she was mentioned at all, it was to say how dear, sweet, good, and ailing poor Lizzie was. Josiah emerged like a rock: he was honest, he was rigid, he was determined, and he carried through what he began. But it was his son, little Robert Josiah Benton, who interested me most.

There was little said about Robert Josiah before 1832, when at ten he was sent away to a school in Massachusetts. There had, of course, been a few references to him earlier. When he was born, Josiah, whose first two children had been girls, wrote proudly to his brother, "My Lizzie was delivered of a fine eight-pound boy this morning. I shall make of him, God willing, a Scholar and a Gentleman." Later on, in one of the few letters that Lizzie seemed to have received, her sister, who had recently been to visit them, exclaimed over what a "Beautiful and Clever child your Robert Josiah is." And once, when Robert Josiah must have been about eight, Josiah's list of expenditures included, "To roan horse for my Son."

Robert Josiah was sent to Massachusetts to be made into a scholar and a gentleman, as Josiah had probably written the headmaster of the school. "According to your instructions," the headmaster replied, "your son will be given a thorough grounding in Mathematics and Latin, with somewhat subordinate attention given to French and to those Sports which befit a Gentleman. You will receive Quarterly Reports from me as to the progress of your Son, and the Rules of our School require that each Scholar shall write his

Father fortnightly so that you shall be well inform'd concerning his Welfare. I personally supervise the writing of these letters, ascertaining that they contain no misleading statements, as the inexperience and frivolity of Youth might give them a tendency to do, so that you shall at all times have a True and Correct account."

Robert Josiah went away to school at the end of the summer, and in the fall and winter months the fortnightly letters appeared, painfully neat, carefully spelled, stiff little letters, beginning, "My Dear and Respected Father"—Lizzie was not addressed, although somewhere in the letter Robert Josiah would say, "Give my Dear Love to my Mother." The letters always ended, "Your obedient Son." He would report that he was well and that he was studying hard in order to gain the full benefits of the advantages that his father was so generously providing for him, that he was treated with the utmost consideration by the professors and by the headmaster, and that he hoped that the headmaster's reports of him would be found to be satisfactory. Once he said that he found Latin very difficult, but he hastened to add, "Do not believe, Dear Father, that I question on this account your Wisdom in desiring me to study it or that I shall Neglect it." Sometimes he apologized for the shortness of a letter by saying, "I am allow'd only one Candle and it is almost finished."

At Christmas he went so far as to say, "I miss

my Dear Mother and you Very much, and my Sisters also, but I shall try to overcome it and to Devote my Attention more fully to my Studies." Often he would inquire about his horse, whose name was Jupiter, and about Nero, his dog. "Does Timothy take good care of Jupiter and of Nero?" he would ask.

And so the letters continued—stiff, polite, adult little notes. But sometimes a barely wistful, faintly childish sound crept into them; once in a while it became perfectly clear that Robert Josiah wanted to come home. In January he failed to write, and instead the headmaster wrote that Robert Josiah was ill with a mild attack of the "Grippe," but felt confident that he would soon be fully recovered. And apparently he was, for two weeks later his letters resumed. But now he wrote once, "I wish I could see my Dear Mother."

Then a letter appeared from John Benton, an older cousin of Robert Josiah's, who was attending Harvard College, and who had had occasion, on returning to college from a short vacation, to stop by Robert Josiah's school.

"My Dear Uncle," he wrote, "I trust that you will forgive the extreme liberty which I am taking in addressing you regarding my recent visit with your Son Robert Josiah. Your Son looks very thin, as a result of his recent bout with the Grippe, and I think perhaps he is studying too hard. I have no doubt that the Headmaster of the School is an extremely Fine and Conscientious Scholar and that his School is an excellent one, but his regime is most Rigorous, and while some boys no doubt profit greatly from this, I think it may be too severe at this stage for Robert Josiah, who is perhaps of delicate constitution and of course of still tender years. I beg to assure you that the attitude of Robert Josiah is one of loving obedience to your wishes, and I trust that you will forgive, my Dear Uncle, this intrusion of mine into your Family Affairs, since I am confident of your Excellent Judgment in all matters. Your respectful Nephew, John Benton."

Well, it was a good thing that somebody had looked in on little Robert Josiah to see how he really was, but the question was, would anyone as determined as Josiah listen?

Apparently not. The weeks passed, and the stiff little letters kept coming from Robert Josiah. But they were more openly homesick now, and once or twice he wandered curiously from the subject as he was writing. Probably John's letter had merely rubbed Josiah the wrong way; he was, after all, only a young upstart of a nephew. Somebody else would have to try to make Josiah understand that Robert Josiah needed to come home—and there was no relying on Lizzie, poor, pale, ailing little thing, probably worried sick but unable to have an opinion about anything. But somebody had to do something! Josiah was not mean; he was just rigid, opinionated, and ambitious; he could be made to understand. Frantically I searched in my mind for the right tack to take with Josiah, the best way to put it to him.

But then something happened—maybe a student going out of the library banged a door—and past and present whirled around me in waves and washed me up at a library table, well into the second half of the twentieth century, with yellow old papers stacked around me. It had all happened in 1832: they were all dead and gone. There was nothing I could do for little Robert Josiah; I could hold in my hand the letters that he had written, and read the words he had put down there, but I was far, far away, separated from him by more than a century. There was nothing I could tell his father; there was no way I could get through from my dimension to his.

Rather halfheartedly I looked for the rest of the letters. There were just two or three more from little Robert Josiah, and then they stopped. There was nothing more. There were accounts, bills, business letters, and, later on, more personal letters to Josiah, but there was nothing mentioning Robert Josiah. I read through thirty or forty more years of Benton papers, but I never saw another word about a son of Josiah Benton's.

III

My cousin Leah and I grew up in different parts of the country and never knew each other well. When she came to live in the city where I now worked, we felt an obligation to be friendly, but the friendliness was a trifle forced, weighted down by our families' expectations that we would have a great deal to say to each other and the inescapable fact that we did not. We rang each other up from time to time to chat and exchange family news, and since she was new to the city I introduced her to my friends. But she was six years younger than I, and the people I knew seemed jaded to her. They were not really jaded at all, but then almost anybody seemed a little battered beside Leah.

Leah's father, my uncle, was old when she was born. His first wife had died, leaving four sons already grown, and eventually he married again, a gentle girl who gave him one daughter and died shortly afterward. People wondered how that stern, hard old man was going to manage with a little girl, but he managed very well. A tender fatherliness flowered in him which his sons had never known. He and Leah were always together; they rode horseback over his farms together, and supervised the haying together, and went shopping for her clothes together, the old man looking as out of place as possible, but calm in the conviction that here, as everywhere else in the world, all you had to do was make it plain what was wanted and be able to pay for it. My uncle was a rich man—not a private-yacht kind of rich, but a Midwest-farming kind of rich, a turn-out-the-lights-when-you're-finished-with-them and don't-dip-into-your-principal kind of rich. When Leah got into her teens and began to be beautiful, he sent her to the best girls' school he could get her into, because he figured their reputation might not mean much, but it was all he had to go on. But first he asked them what they had to teach her that she could earn her living by.

She became a commercial artist, and eventually she came to the city and got a job. The best word I can think of to describe her when I first encountered her, twenty-one, all grown up and on her own, is dazzling. She was radiant; she twinkled and glittered and dazzled like a diamond, yet her strange, pure, golden-brown eyes looked out at the world with the simplicity and delight of a child.

She saw the best in everyone. She met a notorious misogynist and thought him *so* sweet and shy; and she was introduced to a celebrated old lecher and reported that he was so *good* all through that he reminded her a lot of her daddy. She made me nervous. But she was sharing an apartment with two former schoolmates, and the three of them—all as lovely and charming and

gay as if they had been turned out by some heavenly
production line, giggling and putting up each other's
hair and wearing each other's clothes, living off peanut
butter sandwiches and chewing over their combined
worldly wisdom like so many puppies with a shoe—
presented themselves in an invincible girls'-dormitory
armor to the world. And I was, after all, young myself
and in no mood to worry, in love with the city, with my
job in an international organization, and, as I recall it,
with the Third Executive Assistant of the British Dele-
gation.

Then she called me up one night to say that she
was engaged and was going to be married right away.
He was a junior associate in the well-known law firm
of Judd, Parker, and Avery, and his credentials of age,
height, education, and background seemed to be im-
peccable. I felt that she emphasized his suitability a
trifle for my benefit; she put me in the older-relative
category. Her father was not too well; he had recently
had an operation, and she was planning to go home to
see him, and so they had decided to be married here the
following Sunday and to go home together. On Saturday night her roommates were throwing a little party
for them at the apartment, and would I come and meet
Dick then? I said I'd love to, and I wished her all the
happiness in the world.

That was Monday night, and I had such a busy

week that I didn't have much time to think about Leah. A series of international meetings kept me working late every night. On Wednesday I didn't get away until almost midnight, and I was exhausted when I finally caught a cab. I sank back and wiggled out of my high-heeled shoes in the dark. The cabdriver had a girlfriend with him in the front seat; I suppose it's lonely work, cruising the night streets. She leaned against his shoulder, and when he stopped at a red light, he rested his head companionably against her; he said something monosyllabic, and she laughed. I thought wisely, looking at the backs of their heads, that they were too comfortable in their closeness to be a young dating pair, but were old lovers, or married. When we got to my address he turned on the light for a moment to make change. I saw that he was good-looking and probably in his late twenties, and that she was about the same age, pretty, with a mop of blond hair, and in blue jeans.

I must pause here to explain that I am a recognizer of people. I am a sort of Paganini, or Escoffier, of recognizing. People who say, "I remember faces but I just can't remember names," are amateurs; I remember thousands of faces for which I have never known a name. The streets swarm with them: people who once did my hair or sold me shoes, stood next to me in elevators, in ticket lines, or at fires, gave me a new blouse in exchange for one that didn't fit, or four words at a cocktail party in exchange for four of mine. I remember them all; but they cut me dead.

The first time I ever set forth on the streets of Paris, I was with a friend, a woman who occupied a high position in the international organization for which I worked, and who had, as it happened, been mainly responsible for the firing from that organization, a year or so before, of a Frenchman named Charpentier, the reason being general quarrelsomeness, I think. No doubt his side of the story was different; I never knew all the ins and outs of it. He returned to the French civil service, from whence he had come, but not before delivering some fairly painful parting shots.

My friend and I stepped from the boat train out into the spring morning sunshine of Paris, bent on none but pleasant errands, and at once I recognized M. Charpentier on the street. I was used to domestic recognizing; at home I damped down the recognizing smile on my face as automatically as I glanced at the traffic lights; but I lost my head at such a stunning foreign success and cried out, "M. Charpentier!" He stopped, we stopped, and the shock turned both their faces to concrete. He gave a short, savage jerk of a bow, and her teeth met like gears as she ground out a greeting between them. It had been the dearest wish of both their hearts never to see each other again. As the hostess, so to speak, in the situation, I babbled something like "How nice once more to see you again, and how beautiful is your city!," speaking pidgin English, although his own was perfect. He looked at me with a mixture of loathing and bewilderment. We had known each other only slightly a year or more before, and he did not recognize me. My friend and I proceeded on our way, but a shadow had settled over the day. She was rather silent, and I smiled, whenever I caught her eye, Uriah Heepishly. Paris has never been the magic city to me that it is to some.

On Saturday night I went to my cousin's apartment and met her fiancé. He was a good-looking young man in his late twenties, with a conservative tie, a direct eye, and a firm handshake. He greeted me with a special, cousinly warmth, and his manner toward Leah was a charming mixture of serious protectiveness and teasing adoration. And of course he didn't recognize me; there was not the faintest cloud in his clear young gaze. My cousin was radiant: she flitted among the guests like a sprite. "Tell me, Mary," she whispered when she alighted near me for a moment, "what do you think of him? Isn't he *wonderful*? *Isn't* he?"

"He's very handsome and very charming," I said.

"Oh, I'm *so* glad you like him," she cried, and she gave me a hug. "You and Dad are the people I want to like him—I don't care about anybody else!" And she was off.

Well, I suppose that more than one struggling young professional man has driven a cab at night to make a little extra. And surely many a young man has an auld luve to be off wi' before he be on wi' the new—and if the timetable's a bit crowded, it's not a hanging offense. I'm as broad-minded as the next, and yet—and yet—this was my little cousin Leah, my beautiful, shining little cousin, with whom I had not a blessed thing in common, who thought all the world loved her as well as her daddy did. I looked at the young man again, and I imagined that his neatly cut face was clearly sinister and that his every word and gesture was plainly false. Was he really a lawyer with Judd, Parker, and Avery? It would be possible to find out; I could, in fact, simply call them up and ask, on some pretext or other. But it was Saturday night, and the wedding was Sunday, and on Monday I wouldn't want to know.

Or I could, then and there, look him right in the sincere blue eye and tell him that I had seen him driving a cab last Wednesday night with a blond young woman under circumstances suggestive of considerable intimacy, and what, as a promising young lawyer on the eve of marriage to my cousin, did he have to say about it? But how in the name of heaven could I say that? It was melodramatic. It was a line to be delivered by an outraged father, back to the fireplace, or perhaps by a worldly, erect old aunt in her parlor, shooting a severe glance past her teacup. I simply couldn't manage it; I was only a cousin, about his own age and considerably less self-assured than he looked, spectacles slipping woefully down my nose, licensed as neither duenna nor private eye, nervous of making a fool of myself and showing it, in the crush of a large party in a small apartment, where it took a shout to be heard at all, and elbows jostled into conversations from all sides. And, after all, what if I were mistaken? I may be a Paganini, I may be an Escoffier, but the possibility had to be granted, and it would not make a very auspicious beginning for us all. And anyway, it was too late. The chapel was reserved, the wedding dress hung on its satin hanger in the closet, and the organist was instructed to play "I Love You Truly."

When I left that night, I suddenly at the door, without intending to at all, threw my arms around Leah and held her tight. There she was, my little cousin, my equal, my contemporary, within the circle of my arms; but I was separated from her forever by all the complexities of what I did not know and could not do. Our lives carried us on in our own dimensions, like people passing on different escalators, headlong to meet whatever harm or good was to come our way. And so I left her awkwardly, and I smiled jerkily at the bridegroom, who gave me a cousinly peck on the cheek, and we all said something about seeing each other the next day.

I had dinner with them a couple of months later, after they had returned to the city. They seemed very happy, and the stars shone in Leah's eyes as brightly as ever. I couldn't say I liked him; but there was, as I looked him over, this time more quietly and leisurely, something reassuring about his very ordinariness. He simply didn't have the stuff in him to be a Bluebeard or a Landru. He was a bright enough, nice enough young man, who, I surmised, thought his ways to be a little more winning, and other people a little more simple, than they were, and whose eye was firmly fixed on the main chance. But that was the worst I could think of him, and I was glad I hadn't tried to confront him with my silly cab-riding story; it wouldn't have done anyone any good, and perhaps it was all a mistake, anyway. They left the city shortly afterward; Leah called to tell me that an opportunity had opened up for Dick out in the Midwest, and he was leaving Judd, Parker, and Avery. She was glad because she would be nearer her father.

They were divorced about a year later, very shortly after her father died, and my cousin is back in the city, with a job doing fashion-ad illustrations. I assumed she was working just to keep herself busy, but a newsy old aunt of mine who was through town recently tells me that's not so. Leah will be a rich woman, one day, but at present she has to make her living, for her father, just before he died, changed his will so as to tie up the money very securely for a good while to come. I don't know why the divorce, of course—mental cruelty, or something, I suppose; it's nothing I can ask Leah about unless she wants to talk about it. Dick immediately got married again, to a cheap, fuzzy-headed little blonde, as my aunt puts it. Leah's still a handsome woman, but the dazzle is gone, and she looks tired around the eyes. But so do I; so, in time, does everybody.

The Infant

She lay in bed, in a fury with Roger. Her feet were cold, bitterly cold, and although she rubbed them together and raised them carefully in the air, bringing them down smartly to catch the covers in a close nest about them, to make what she called, when she was a child, a foothouse, and tried to take her mind off them, on the theory that they would eventually warm up, it did no good. They were cold, miserably cold. They were always cold; in fact, she was always cold. Her temperature was practically never up to the standard 98.6; it was low metabolism or something, no doubt. Or sluggish blood. She always visualized the bloodstream as, indeed, a stream, winding along through hilly and eccentric country; and her own she thought of as rather greenish in color and indolent, settling down torpidly in puddles.

Roger, on the other hand, always seemed to be running a slight temperature. He was hot; his face was always flushed and hot; his feet radiated heat, like a Franklin stove, so that five inches away you could feel the glow; his bloodstream coursed from one to the other in a wild, headlong dash.

By lifting her head to free both ears from the pillows, and straining intently, she could just barely hear the television downstairs, which Roger was listening to. It made her furious. She considered going downstairs and telling him so. She considered stalking in and saying, "Up the way I am every night with that child, the one night I do get a chance to go to bed at a decent hour, I do think that the least you could do is to turn off that television so I could get some sleep. But I'm sure that wouldn't occur to you."

She recognized that this would probably make him mad; he would probably say that he had it turned very low and he didn't believe she could hear it. He might be quite nasty about it.

She decided that the mature thing to do was to go down and say, "You know, Roger, that television does bother me, just a little. So perhaps as soon as you're finished with this program you'd skip it for the rest of the evening, unless there's something special you want to see. Actually, you ought to be getting to bed anyway—you do look a bit tired, dear."

She saw herself bending over and kissing him lightly on the forehead, in a mature, but sexy, way.

Suddenly she realized that she didn't seem to hear the television anymore. She raised her head and listened, intensely. It was gone. She was furious; he was *probably* reading now. She peered out the door to see if she could see a crack of light wending its way from downstairs; there was one, although it was very pale. "Roger," she said to herself, "I hate to bother you, but that light *is* keeping me awake, you know . . ."

Well. She smiled a little, beginning to feel sleepy. That *was* pretty feeble. Suddenly she realized that her feet were almost thawed out, and, at last, she slept.

Margaret lay, her arms flung out and her skin firm and brown in the moonlight with her hair in a long dark drift down her back. On the little table beside her bed was a glass of water, resting on a neatly folded square of Kleenex, and with another neatly folded square of Kleenex on top of it; a bottle of hay fever pills, for she once in a while got an attack of sneezing in the middle of the night; and the alarm clock; and under the bed were her blue slippers, facing the bed, at odd angles. Roger slept, too, the covers thrown back, for he was hot; and beside him was a small container of pleasant mint-flavored pills, in case his stomach bothered him during the night, and the book he was currently reading, in case he should be wakeful and want to get up and read it during the night; his brown leather slippers, under the bed, stood at attention, side by side, and facing outward, ready for action, and his dressing gown hung neatly over the arm of the chair that stood near the foot of the bed.

Each of them had hung his pack over his shoulder, a few things that gave him courage for the trip, and set out on the strange, long journey of sleep; knowing that though he might see some of the others on his way, the journey would be his, and he would be traveling alone.

Henry sat up in bed reading late, for they had forgotten to turn off his light. Henry was almost two, and what he was reading was an illustrated brochure of suggested Christmas gifts put out by a department store. He laid a forefinger on the picture of a silver vase; he felt tentatively around the edges of the vase, not really hopefully, for he had already learned that it was difficult to pick them up off the page, but with the air of giving it one more try. He sighed and turned the page and saw the picture of a stuffed horse with a tasseled mane, and he said softly to himself, "Woof-woof."

The reason they had forgotten to turn off his light was that the baby was crying. In the distance he heard faintly the angry, panicky squawls of the baby, and he listened to it incuriously and objectively. He knew exactly what was taking place in the room where the baby was; his mental picture of it was clear, precise, and full of detail. He had no words for it all; it was simply a picture, appearing at once before his mind's eye, clear, precise, a picture taken from about two feet off the floor. Either his mother or his father was walking around carrying the baby over one shoulder; the little red face looked over the shoulder angrily, with wrinkled brow, and the mouth wide open in protest. His mental picture included the fact that the light was on, and the position of the light switch, for he was very interested in light switches; the silver rattle on the dresser, which he coveted.

The Hamiltons came at four one afternoon. Margaret supposed that they came to see the baby, but he was asleep, and she didn't offer to wake him; perhaps he would wake up anyway pretty soon. She sat, bone-weary, on the couch and talked to them; she half wished that they would go away so she could lie down and go to sleep, but at the same time it was nice to sit and talk.

The Hamiltons were going to have a baby soon,

their first, and they were very interested in the subject of babies. May Hamilton, shifting herself in her chair, said, "Well, I envy you, with the baby here and you nice and slim again. Are you taking exercises to get your figure back in shape?" Margaret allowed her mind to settle on and consider the ache in her back, the ache in her arms from holding the baby all night long, the ache in her knees from climbing the stairs, the heavy weariness in her legs, the sick dull feeling all through her of lack of sleep. "Well, no, I'm not," she said. "I don't seem to get around to it. The baby's been awfully fussy and I just don't seem to get around to it."

Paul Hamilton blinked behind his horn-rimmed glasses and said, "You know, at six weeks they relive the birth trauma. That's probably all it is."

"Do you feel you're anxious with the baby?" asked May.

"You did have rooming-in, didn't you?" asked May. "Wasn't it simply *won*derful, getting acquainted with the baby, and having him right there with you, and *shar*ing everything with him from the first day?"

Something rose up in Margaret. "No," she said flatly, "I think it's terrible."

Paul and May leaned forward, startled. "What do you *mean*?" they asked.

"Well," Margaret said, "I think there are a few times in life when a person should relax and be taken care of, and I think when you've just had a baby is one of them. I don't want to crawl out of bed in the middle of the night when I feel wobbly as hell and change my squalling newborn baby's diapers, and I don't want to spend the night listening to my neighbor's rooming-in baby squall in the next room. I'm going to be taking care of this child for the next fifteen or twenty years, and I want somebody to take care of me and him both for a few days until I feel able to sail into this assignment. I'm tired and worn out, and if I ever have another baby I'm going to hunt up some old-fashioned doddering alcoholic obstetrician who hasn't read a book or been to a medical convention in forty years and who will tell me I'm to stay flat on my back and not move for two weeks after he's born, and see him only when he's in a good humor."

The Hamiltons left, bug-eyed. Margaret fancied she could hear them beginning on their way to the car, "She is really a rejecting mother . . . no maternal feeling at all . . . no wonder she's already having difficulty with that baby."

They were all asleep, and no one heard the baby when he awoke again and cried softly, whimperingly. But it was just as well, for no one could really help him; he cried because he had just emerged from the sleepy depths of the newborn and learned something—learned that he was alone, and finite; that he was no longer really close to anyone else, immersed in another; but that where his hands and feet and belly ended the outside world began, a great misty void, in which fuzzy figures came closer, sometimes, and then dissolved again, leaving only the void. He ached with the emptiness into which he was thrust, the aloneness that was his lot.

Later Margaret sat rocking him; every bone in her body ached, and her eyes felt strained with the intensity of keeping them open. She looked at the little gnomelike figure in her lap, and she thought, I suppose he'll be cute when he's two, and we shall be terribly proud of him and wouldn't be able to imagine life without him, but all I can think of now is that *I wish we hadn't had him.*

Suddenly she was full of compunction. The tears rolled down her face, and she snatched him closer, fiercely defending him. "Never mind," she told him. "You've got a right to be a baby, too!"

Penelope

All winter Jane played with Penelope. She had other dolls, but she didn't like them so well, because they were big, common, sprawling, babyish dolls, while Penelope was about four inches tall and a lady. Her name was Penelope with the accent on the first syllable and rhyming approximately with cantaloupe; later Jane discovered that an odd, out-of-joint pronunciation seemed to be generally well thought of, but at this period no doubts had yet arisen.

Penelope was a princess, and she didn't live in Texas, and when she was a child she had never picked cotton, and she hadn't wiped dishes, and she had never roasted the spines off cactus to feed to the cows, winters when there wasn't enough feed. Since she was little she could have a satin dress because Jane's grandmother's good slip had been shortened, with a lace train that had once been sombody's cuff, and she could have brocade because the insides of the menfolks' ties sometimes did not fade and wear with the rest, and she could have pearls and velvet and rubies and *everything,* all because she was so little. She was the king's daughter in the fairy story, the lady in the Lux soap ads, she was Guinevere and the fainting beauty right out of Scott, and sewing women had toiled for years over her gowns, and brave divers had dived to the bottoms of the seven seas for her pearls, and she would never, never have dishpan hands.

Summer came and the cotton season was on, and the sky was hot and blue. Orange or gray or red wagons of bright white cotton pulled slowly down the roads past the Holmeses' house in a great procession. The gins in the little town a mile or so away churned monotonously all day and all night, and the great piles of cotton hulls mounted in their yards and then were reduced to nothing in big bonfires and mounted again, and the cotton bales were stacked on the platforms by the rail siding and then sold and shipped away. The cotton buyers were about, citified men from Corpus

Christi and Houston and even St. Louis and New Orleans, who smoked cigars and drank Cokes in Bresnahan's drug store. The local men who loafed around in front of Gibson's general store said, "Robins passed a thousand bales today"; or "The Old Smith Gin is just at its five hundredth bale"; or "The Farm Bureau is gaining on Robins"—taking an immense delight in the commerce and the competition and the enterprise of the season, because most of the year there wasn't much of anything to talk about.

Now the long months of waiting for the cotton season were past, the months when people had bought their cottonseed, and prepared their ground, and planted their cottonseed, and wondered if they would have a stand, and chopped the cotton, and hoped passionately for rain and then desperately for drought, and negotiated for cotton pickers, and dickered over wages, and hired their sisters-in-law for cotton weighers and their nephews to drive the wagons to the gin, and indulgently promised their little girl children a dollar a hundred pounds for all they could pick . . . the months when gin owners had sent to Tennessee for a new fan belt, and oiled the machinery, and discussed with their wives whether the brightest high-school boy would be good for a bookkeeper or might be too smart for his pants, and acted extra cordial toward landowners or renters, according to which one of them, on each farm, decided where the cotton was to be ginned.

It was all past, and the cotton season was here, and the first bale in the county had long since been ginned free of charge and wrapped in its tidy burlap casing and been bought at a premium by the cotton buyers. People didn't talk anymore about whether they would make a crop or seem to worry anymore about barefoot children and unpaid mortgages and empty flour barrels, as they had earlier in the year. "Roger made half a bale to the acre on that little piece of his next to the highway," they observed briefly. "He sent away and got Quala seed."

One day about the middle of cotton season a little boy named Jesus came to the Holmeses' front door with a little basket with a polite request to buy un dimé worth of eggs. He was the son of Young Teodoro and the grandson of Old Teodoro, all of whom lived together in a two-room house with an assortment of gourds, peppers, and goat's meat nailed to the front doorpost for drying, and a roof made of tin cans, and a little yard with hibiscus and hound dogs growing in it.

Standing there at the front door, he looked like a little aristocrat, which he was, with his delicate nose curved like a Spanish grandee's, and his fine black eyes set under arched black brows, and his graceful bare foot thoughtfully resting against his slender brown leg, and his sleeves gaping at the elbows, and one patrician hand holding a woven basket and the other massaging a thin Roosevelt dime.

Jane's mother liked to sell a few eggs, as the capable Leghorn hens laid more than she could really use, and anyway she rather relished the sensation of money coming in. So she went to the kitchen to get the eggs and Jane followed her.

"As soon as it's cotton season and the Mexicans get a little money for picking cotton, they want eggs," Jane's mother said, setting a big basket of eggs on the oilcloth-covered kitchen table.

"What do they live on in winter when it isn't cotton season?" Jane asked, leaning her elbows on the edge of the table.

"They eat dried frijole beans and tortillas," her mother said.

"Don't they mind?" Jane said.

"They like beans," her mother said.

"How many eggs will the little boy get?" Jane said.

"Well," said her mother, looking up the market page of the *San Antonio Express*, "eggs are selling at 23.7 cents per dozen. The first thing is to find how much one egg is worth." So she tried dividing 12 into 23.7, but it wouldn't go.

"You should be able to figure that out."

"I'm not good at arithmetic," Jane said.

"I think the way to do it is like this. 23.7 is to 12 as 10 is to x."

Jane worked on it awhile, and came out with 24. Finally, she asked, "How many are there in Old Teodoro's family?"

"I don't know," said her mother. "I guess ten or eleven part of the time. Some of the sons aren't much good and are always coming home."

"Why don't you give Jesus a few extra eggs?" Jane asked.

"Where do you think your piano lessons come from?" her mother said.

"Oh," Jane said.

Then Jane's mother was caught up by a qualm, for she was a woman of scrupulously honest intentions. She picked out nine lovely large white eggs, which were packed in Jesus's little basket, and she told Jane to take them to him and put the dime in the little glass on the kitchen shelf. Jane walked to the screen door where Jesus stood, leaning his brown nose against the screen and looking with his shiny black eyes into the living room. She couldn't tell what he was looking at—the scrubbed bare boards of the farmhouse floor and the pretty braided rugs Grandmother had made of their old clothes, or the homemade bookcases with Shakespeare and Jerome K. Jerome and Hawthorne and

Harold Bell Wright leaning crookedly on each other, or the old upright piano in the corner—or whether he was looking at nothing at all. His eyes were so shiny and black that you couldn't tell. She noticed that he was a very thin little boy and that his shirt was so torn that it could never be mended so as to hold together again. She couldn't keep from thinking about the nine eggs and how Old Teodoro's older sons, even though they were not much good, might like an egg, now in the cotton season.

She gave the eggs to Jesus, and he gave her the dime he had been holding tightly in his hand, and he said gracias in a polite little voice, bowing from the waist, for no transaction was too trifling to merit the utter courtesy of a son of Young Teodoro. Her mother frequently said that the Mexicans were a very polite people.

"Do you have a little sister?" she asked suddenly.

"Sí," Jesus said, not moving his black eyes at all.

"Does she like dolls?"

"Sí," he said again.

"Wait a minute," she said, and she snatched up Penelope and pressed her and all twelve of her dresses, including the satin with the train, into Jesus's hands. "Will you give her this?" she said. "Be *sure* and give them to her."

"Sí," said Jesus, exactly as he had said it before.

When Jesus was gone, she ran to get her baseball, and she called Phoenix, the dog, to see whether he'd retrieve it when she threw it. Some days he would and some days he wouldn't. She hoped Jesus really did have a sister and that he understood what she meant for him to do with Penelope; sometimes they just said sí whether they understood a thing you said or not. And of course maybe little Mexican boys were just as hateful as the little boys she went to school with and would as soon throw Penelope away as not. But she didn't worry much about it. A baseball was really more fun, in summer.

Boys

The first smell of summer was in the air. Or perhaps it was really the sounds—the after-school sounds of children's voices, which had been imprisoned inside all winter, and then, until that first still afternoon, blown away upon the spring winds. The last daffodils still bloomed along the picket fence, and on the front porch the baby slept in his carriage, his eyes shut tight against the first summer sun he had ever known.

She had gone back to the kitchen for something when she heard the knock at the front door. There stood a little boy, perhaps seven years old, with wide, alarmed eyes.

"Me and my friend are going home from school," he said in a burst, "and there's some Big Boys down there won't let us go past"—he waved toward a wooded patch, perhaps several hundred yards away, where there was a rocky little stream. "Would you please come and make them let us alone?"

She looked down at him, and the fright in her eyes met the fright in his.

"Do you know the Big Boys?" she asked, sparring for time.

"I never saw them before in *my life!*" he said righteously.

Suddenly she didn't feel grown up at all; she felt seven years old—no, it must have been six; she was in the first grade, and she walked home from school across a little woodsy place. And there were some *Big Boys*—big, powerful, fearsome creatures who stopped her and tormented her and would not let her pass. One of them threw a couple of rocks at her, and another one snatched her knitted woolen cap—it had bright red and green and yellow stripes running around it, and a big red pom-pom on top—and threw it high on a thorny bush. She believed that they had laughed at her while, sobbing, her hands torn by the thorns, struggling among the scratchy branches, she managed to get it down from the bush, for she could not go home without it. And always afterward she had gone home shaking with fear that the Big Boys might appear again. Had they ever stopped her again, or was it only that one time? She couldn't remember, but she knew that she had sought out new routes in the hope that she might elude them. They had been like the evil trolls in the children's story who lived under the bridge and tormented people who had to cross it; she had never been able to imagine that they had homes, or that they had ever been little boys, or that they had ever later become men. Even now she could not imagine what they had thought they were doing, or what the point of it was to them; she could not imagine any conversation between them that sounded like the conversation of real people. They were a mystery; they were large symbols of sheer, senseless terror. Other male beings had lost any sense of mystery they had once had for her; her Uncle Albert, the grocery-store man, the sulky boy behind the soda fountain, the convicted rapist in the newspapers, her ninth-grade algebra teacher, even, sometimes, her husband—with all of them she fancied that she had some inkling of what they had in mind. But with the Big Boys, never.

But the little boy was looking up at her trustingly.

"Where do you live?" she asked.

"Way over there." He waved vaguely.

"Do you always come home this way?"

"No'm," he said. "But I came home this way one

time a long time ago, and I saw the little stream, and I wanted to show it to my friend."

"Where is your friend now?" she asked.

"He's still over there where the Big Boys are."

She had reached the end of her resources; all the facts seemed to be in, and she could no longer avoid offering a solution of some kind. But the things that came to her didn't seem very suitable. She felt like telling him that she didn't know what he should do, but if he ever figured it out, she wished he would come and tell her. But she couldn't say that; he would think it very queer, coming from an adult. Or she might tell him that the only thing to do about it was to grow up as fast as possible; somehow, after you yourself got bigger, you didn't seem to have this sort of encounter with Big Boys anymore. But that wouldn't do either; growing up seems like a hopelessly long process when you're seven.

"Well, I'll tell you," she said at last, trying to sound very wise, "if those Big Boys want to act like bullies, it's just a waste of time to argue with them. Why don't you and your friend just go home a different way this afternoon, and some other time when the Big Boys aren't around, you can show your friend the stream."

"But," he said, struggling to convey the enormity of it to her, "they won't let us take our bicycles." This was serious; it involved property. Sadly she conceded that she could not retreat, for you simply could not go home without your bicycle, any more than you could go home without your red and green and yellow cap with the pom-pom.

"Well," she said, gathering up her courage, "I'll go with you and see that they let you get your bicycles." She glanced at the baby. He would be all right; he was still sleeping peacefully.

They set off for the stream, and again she saw the Big Boys in the distance—large, ominous, dangerous figures, high on the opposite bank. Nonsense, she told herself, they're probably no more than eleven years old, and, after all, I'm a grown woman. It suddenly occurred to her that she had not checked one important point with the little boy.

"Did they throw rocks at you?" she asked.

"No'm. We threw rocks at them; they deserved it," he said virtuously.

A chill came over her feelings for him; she looked down at him coldly, as a lawyer might look at a client whose case, as they are proceeding into court, suddenly develops some major flaws. There had been no flaws in her own case, she thought righteously; her conduct had been beyond reproach; she had strictly minded her own business; and she had been quite unquestionably an innocent victim. There had been no provocation—unless, she thought suddenly, one could consider that red and green and yellow cap, which her grandmother had knitted for her, and which *was* rather glaring. But surely no reasonable being would look upon that as provocation; and yet—she was lost in the old puzzle—what was reasonable to a Big Boy?

But there was no turning back now; from the opposite bank, the Big Boys and the one little boy watched their approach; the two bicycles lay on the ground between them. She and the little boy came to the stream, which was almost dry, but the bed was deep and rocky, and the opposite bank was quite perpendicular. The little boy leaped nimbly from rock to rock and scrambled up the other side, and she started to follow him, but she thought better of it. She had a very strong feeling that one must avoid making a fool of oneself in front of Big Boys, and falling from one of those pointed rocks into the stream, or starting up the opposite bank and not being able to make it, would most certainly make her lose face disastrously. She took up as commanding a position as possible on the bank; she planted her feet rather far apart, put her hands on her hips, held her head at a high, severe angle, and attempted to look quite menacing. But instead of picking up their bicycles and departing under benefit of her convoy, the little boys, feeling quite bold now, seemed disposed to fall into an extended discussion of the situation. She was too far away to hear what they said, but their attitudes were aggressive. She raised up her voice and shouted, "You little boys take your bicycles and go right straight home now."

They looked at her in an injured way; it was not the glorious ending they had anticipated. But reluctantly they picked up their bicycles and started off, looking back regretfully. She stood there and watched until they were out of sight; and the Big Boys sat down on the bank and tossed pebbles into the stream with exaggerated indifference.

As she walked home, it came to her: She had been wrong all these years; Big Boys were not simply an entity, a mysterious, isolated group of beings with no beginnings and no future. Little boys grew and became Big Boys—and what was in their minds, heaven alone knew. Why, then, perhaps *men* were really—no, no, she thought, trying to push back the rising hysteria, trying to evoke the familiar, the perfectly reasonable and understandable images of Uncle Albert, the old fellow behind the grocery-store counter, her brother, her husband.

She went up the front steps and looked into the carriage on the porch to see if the baby was all right, and he stirred in his sleep, opened his eyes, and gave her a sweet, innocent, simple smile. She started to smile back, but then she looked at him again, and it seemed to her that there was a mysterious look in his eye, a look quite beyond any understanding—the look of a *boy;* and terror rose in her.

As even the most earnest student longs for graduation, the most faithful employee yearns for retirement, so Martha Hedges looked forward to widowhood. She would not by word or deed have attempted to hasten such an outcome; this is not a murder story. On the contrary, she was a devoted wife who lived in loving concord with a genuinely good husband. Being, in her shy and quiet way, a devout woman, she expected eventually to rejoin Harold in Heaven for all eternity; but she counted on a nice long vacation first.

She did not know herself how much she wanted to be a widow. A housewife's life is such that she may spend a good deal of time in daydreams that are scattered as quickly as they are assembled, so that she hardly knows she had them. When she woolgathers over the kitchen sink, people do not tiptoe past, forbearing to interrupt her preoccupation; instead they say loudly, "What have you done with my old blue jacket?" And what she was thinking is gone so swiftly that she never knows she thought it. The dream she entertained as she dawdled over the frozen vegetables is sent flying at the checkout counter, the vision she saw as she vacuumed is sent into oblivion by the man who reads the gas meter, and the scene that flickered before her eyes as she mended is turned off by the sudden thought that it's time to get the roast in.

Even when Martha's dream was so vivid that the fringes of it stayed with her later, she dismissed it on the grounds that one can't help but think about these things sometimes; her husband was eight years older than she; a number of the older women of her acquaintance were widows. It did no harm to face such facts occasionally. You couldn't call it morbid.

She knew that Harold was an excellent husband. She had never tearfully beckoned him home from the door of a barroom, for he did not drink to excess. She had never lacked for money to pay the milkman, for he earned a good income and managed it wisely. And she had never found lipstick on his shirt, for he was a man of outstanding faithfulness. Sometimes when a friend confided a tale of a philandering husband, her eyes brightened, for she was a thoroughly kind and generous woman, and she took real pleasure in the good fortune of others. On the rare occasions when Harold worked late in the office, the circumstantial evidence that he had done so was overwhelming, among which was Harold himself, home by ten o'clock, tired, irascible, and hungry. He made business trips out of town occasionally, and one would have thought, surely . . . But no; he phoned practically every evening. His voice, which had an odd quality of carrying over the wires with peculiar naturalness and clarity from Montreal, or Louisville, or San Francisco, came through loud and strong, wanting to know whether she had told the roof man what he had told her to tell him, whether the cleaners had found his tan raincoat, and whether she had remembered to prune the forsythia.

She was also fortunate in her three sons, at this time almost grown and a credit to their parents, with lively minds and wholesome interests. John was quick and strong and athletic. Arithmetic had been hard for him when he was a little boy, and evening after evening she had sat with him over his homework, trying to help him to discover the answers for himself, and she had invented number games to play with him, and used the pattern in the kitchen linoleum to explain the Pythagorean theorem. Now he was becoming an engineer, and he was very good at mathematics, and he smiled at hers. Dashing in to change his clothes, he would see her sitting worriedly at her desk, with bills and checkbook and budget book and bank statement spread out around her (Harold liked everything kept track of), and he would laugh affectionately and say, "Having trouble making the pesky little figures behave, Mom?" And he would add, as he rushed off with his tennis racket under his arm, "You will remember about taking Ginger to the vet for his shots, won't you, Mom?"

James was thin and intense and literary. He had loved books from the time he was a little thing, and, loving them herself, she had rediscovered all the dear old stories with him. With Mark Twain they learned to pilot a steamboat, and Mr. Bixby's round and polished curses rose on the evening air and then sank like stones into the blue waters of the Mississippi. In the mythic byways of ancient Phrygia, that devoted old couple, Baucis and Philemon, spread on a clean coarse cloth a frugal meal for the stranger who came to their humble door. And when he told them that he was Jupiter, and that he would grant them one wish, they wished, since they had passed their whole lives together in concord, that the same hour might take them both from life, and neither should live to see the other's grave. She and James had not a dry eye between them, and they turned with a happy sigh to *The Swiss Family Robinson*.

Now, at nineteen, James was the editor of a literary

review, mimeographed. The staff of the review often met in their living room, gathered on the floor at James's feet, while he, the charisma rising from him like steam, narrowed his eyes penetratingly and gestured thoughtfully with his pipe. At any rate, they lay on the floor, but their feet were generally up, on the best sofa. Martha tried to keep out of the way, but she need not have bothered, for to the staff she was like the paper on the wall, a silver-gray stripe, no doubt, with cabbage roses, sweet but tacky. When she expressed interest in seeing the review, James said he didn't think she would care for it; it was pretty experimental and advanced. As he dashed off to supervise the proofreading, he shouted back to her, "Mom, would you mind calling the dentist and breaking my appointment for this afternoon? Can't make it."

Roger was very musical. She had served as the audience for his practicing for years, calling out from the kitchen how marvelously he did his new piece, except for that *one* little hard spot. And now he was seventeen, and when he was not playing the piano or the organ or the recorder, he played medieval plainsongs on the record player. Sometimes, for a change, he put on "Jesu, Joy of Man's Desiring," and he listened to it over and over, admiring its subtleties and studying its construction. The reiterative, contrapuntal never-letting-well-enough-alone beat on her brain like a fever, and she tried to be out doing the marketing a good deal. His girlfriend wore black stockings, and her long straight hair hung in front of her face like a curtain at intermission. As they dashed off to their madrigal-singing group, Roger called back over his shoulder, "Oh, I forgot to tell you, Mom, I asked a few of the kids to come for supper after rehearsal."

The dentist was called up and stalled off with an unlikely story, and now she was on her way to the vet's, Ginger leaning his large head out of the back window and barking at the traffic. She considered supper. When was after rehearsal? Seven-thirty, nine, eleven? What would be delectable at seven-thirty, creditable at nine, and still edible at eleven? Fried chicken? And how many was a few? Two, five, or fifteen? The number that comprised a few was fluctuant and mutable, but the number of pieces in a chicken was not: seven, not counting necks and gizzards. Meanwhile, the dream silently assembled itself and hovered before her eyes, just beyond the windshield wipers. She saw herself all alone in her widowhood, her three sons married to suitable girls, living some distance away. She planned to be perfectly lovely to her daughters-in-law, and to leave them strictly alone, for young people need their privacy. As a matter of fact, she intended to be perfectly lovely to her daughters-in-law even if they were not too suitable. At a stoplight, Ginger tried to attack a truck, and a shudder went through her; it came to her that they might turn out to be old bachelors, living at home.

They smiled, all of them, at her flustered, breathless, worrisome way of going about her household tasks. Every facility of modern suburban housekeeping was hers, to say nothing of her weekly cleaning woman, which made her little inefficiencies the more absurd. She had eighteen different kinds of soaps and detergents to aid her, for the soap that was catnip to the washing machine was ptomaine to the dishwasher; the soap that cleaned John's hands after he had worked on his car was not the soap that was wanted for baths, and neither was the thing for washing the dog. The inside and the outside of the refrigerator required different substances, and the waxes were separate and distinct for tile floors, wood floors, asphalt floors, for chrome, for furniture, and for porcelain. The papers— extra-strength, linenlike, waxed, coated, bug-repelling, and petal-soft—multiplied around her. By the kitchen telephone hung a list of numbers, of the skilled and specialized, the reliable and trustworthy, who would at her bidding speed over freeway and past shopping center, around cloverleaf and through dangerous intersection, and, arriving, speak learnedly to her of the washer in the faucet and the baffle in the washer, the gasket in the freezer and the toggle in the dryer, the impeller, the deflector, the main drive pinion, and the intermediate-frequency amplifier. If she had called them earlier, at the first hint of the grinding sound in the motor, the odd lacelike stitch of the sewing machine, the tinniness of the A above middle C, and the bit of moisture on the floor, the damage would not have gone so far, nor be so expensive to repair; but they said they would do what they could. A sigh that was nearly a sob would escape her. Harold bought only the best, but then he expected it to do its duty, and repair bills upset him dreadfully. She sighed for the long, laborious hours of work on the accounts that lay ahead of her, to make this expenditure disappear without a trace. Whenever she read in the papers of some embezzling accountant who had falsified his records for years, her soft heart would go out to him; she knew what hard, tedious work it was.

Despite her best efforts, something inevitably went wrong with the household, for her mind was like a computer whose cards have been punched too often. The most recently summoned specialist came, at the time he had said he could not possibly come, while she was away getting the kind of soap they were out of, and he went away in a huff. The system broke down, and if the lack or failure was one that could not be concealed from her menfolk, despite the most careful management and even deception, they reproached her. She had, on a few occasions, managed to deploy two rolls of paper over three bathrooms, by watchful vigilance, swift and silent legwork, and astute timing; they would have been incredulous at the idea that people engaged with things that really mattered should be troubled by so ridiculous a lack.

Her uncle Theodore died, and although Martha was not able to go to the funeral, for Harold had a virus, she begged her aunt Alice to come and stay with her for a while after it was all over. When Aunt Alice arrived, they clasped each other wordlessly, the tears running down both their faces; Aunt Alice had been married forty years to Uncle Theodore, and it was as if half of her self was gone. Martha had always been fond of her uncle, an upright man with a heart of gold, although a trifle loud around the house; and her feelings were so tender that her aunt's loss was as if it were her own. They sat in the days that followed and pored over the suitcaseful of sympathy cards and letters that Aunt Alice had brought along, leaving them to face until she could do so with Martha. "Theodore was a man of exemplary character, and his passing is a grievous loss not only to his family but to the whole community." "We know that you are comforted by the knowledge that you have shared life's road with a saintly man, of generous heart and noble spirit." "Even in your hour of sorrow, it must be a great comfort to you to look back upon your years of joyful marriage to a man as thoughtful and understanding as Theodore." "Theodore was always cheerful, always helpful, always ready to listen to another's troubles, and wherever he went he brought sunshine," Martha read, and her ready tears came again. "Uncle Theodore *was* a dear, good man," she said. But her aunt's eyes had dried momentarily. "I know he was, I know he was," she said a little testily. "But do you suppose all these people really think it was just one long picnic to live with Theodore for forty years?" And she began to weep again.

They put the cards away, still slightly moist from their tears, and turned to other things. Aunt Alice said that she planned to have the bedroom painted when she returned home; it had been blue for so long. They settled on a pale, daffodil yellow, and bought a new rug, and looked for drapery material, and tried to keep busy and cheerful. Aunt Alice had, of course, her despairing moments, when she said that she doubted she would survive poor Theodore long; but she was taking vitamin pills, and making sure to get all the trace elements.

And as she shopped with Aunt Alice and took her to the theater, and tried to think of things to keep her occupied, Martha's dream hung about in the wings, and took a brief turn on the stage now and then, almost unnoticed. Aunt Alice would go back to her big old two-story frame house, with its shady porch and white wooden lace and big, cool yard. It was home, and she could not imagine living anywhere else. One's home was, of course, home; still, for herself, Martha thought of a small, spartan apartment, just big enough for one, with nothing that barked or miaowed or swam or had moving parts, except, perhaps, a telephone, on which very occasionally she would call an old friend to make a date for lunch, or the lending library to see whether they had the latest book. The sofa would go along the long wall, and the little desk in the corner. . . .

One grew old, Martha had often noticed, not in a smooth, imperceptible, continuous process, as the hands of a good watch move, but in sudden jerks, like an old-fashioned alarm clock. One seemed to stay in one place for a long while, time standing still, as good as one ever was; and then, all at once, a slow recovery from a case of flu coincided with the chairmanship of the library fund drive, with sixteen out-of-town colleagues of Harold's to dinner, a slightly wrenched back, and a few depressing remarks by the dentist, and one had suddenly lurched ahead a notch.

That was what Martha thought it was—the vague malaise, the indefinite ailing—that summer of her fifty-fourth year. But it was more, for even though the doctors themselves did not realize it at first, she had been stricken by a rare, swift, and deadly disease. Suddenly she was in the hospital, and through the mist of pain and unease and sedation she knew, though no one told her, that she was terribly ill. But worse than that knowledge was something else that nagged at her—some emotion so unfamiliar that she could not even identify it. She had always been sentimental for others to the point of foolishness; but for herself, things didn't matter; she had always been a good sport, a stoic, an optimist. So the feeling that came over her now was quite unknown to her; it was the simple, painful sensation of being cheated. She had wanted something; she had expected it, counted on it, and it was being denied her. But, lying in her hospital bed, among the white shapes that came and murmured and went away, she could not remember what it was.

She remembered one evening when her sons were gathered around her bed—Harold had been sent away to get some rest. All of a sudden a great clarity came to her about what her trouble was, what it was that was being done to her, and knowing, dimly, who they were, it seemed to her that perhaps they would understand. Bringing out her words with effort, and with a loud, blunt definiteness that was quite unlike her, she said, *"I didn't want to die first."* She never spoke again.

The remark sounded on in their ears in the days that followed. John said to himself that she was, of course, delirious. Roger pushed it out of his mind, for he was miserable enough as it was. But James thought a good deal about it.

By unspoken consent they did not repeat it to their father, for he was in no state to cope with enigmas. Harold was, in fact, in bad shape. He was overcome by grief and by grievance, in roughly equal proportions. He had never known Martha to be disloyal, but he had always sensed in her a subtle capacity to be. More than once, when he had made some normal, everyday remark to her, such as had she remembered to have the oil, tires, and battery water checked when she got gas, her eyes had seemed to focus on him slowly, as if she were returning from a distance, from the other half of a double life. It was as if she had always reserved something; as if she had it in her to go off headlong on some independent course of action, without consulting him. And he had been right. She had gone ahead and died without discussing it with him, and without a thought of his welfare and happiness.

On the evening of the funeral, when all the friends and relatives had gone at last, and Harold had been given a little something to make him sleep, the boys were sitting, restless and morose in each other's company, in the living room. Breaking the silence, James knocked out his pipe and said quietly,

"You know, of course, what she meant, don't you?"

"No. I suppose you do?" said John heavily.

"I will tell you," said James. "Mother was essentially a very simple person, and most of our interests and even Dad's meant little to her. But she was also a truly great person, for she had the gift of perfect devotion. Her only happiness was in taking care of those she loved. And she was like Baucis in the myth; the only thing she asked for was not to go before Dad did, for she knew how lonely and lost he would be without her. Her dream was that neither of them would live to see the other's grave, as the story goes. The reason I know is that I remember vividly how the tears ran down her face as she read the story of Baucis and Philemon to me when I was a boy."

As he spoke, John and Roger raised their faces, and the sadness and despair disappeared, and they became transfixed and aglow. They had loved their mother, and they would miss her sorely, but they would never have guessed that her life had ended on a note of such classic beauty. Throughout their lives, Martha's sons cherished her last words, and they often mentioned them to their wives.

Lois

in the

Country

Driving out to the country for a Sunday at the Holmeses' place, Lois was hoping that nothing very awful would happen. The Holmeses were so loud, and sometimes the Holmes children would play the piano very noisily for hours, and other times they would hardly bother to look up from the books they were reading. Last time, the Holmeses had talked about contagious abortion, which was something the cows might catch, they said, and about cow serums and other matters. Of course, the Holmeses were farmers, but it did seem as if even farmers could draw the line somewhere, especially in front of one's little girls.

The rows of whatever it was in the fields along the highway seemed to be spinning by very quickly. "August"—she turned to her husband—"aren't you driving quite fast, dear?"

"Just forty-five, Lois," he said irritably, just as if she couldn't see by the speedometer that he was going over fifty. It was best not to argue with him.

She could never make up her mind whether August and his sister, Em Holmes, were much alike or not. August seemed entirely different from Em and all the Holmeses when he was in the city, dressed in his neat suits, coming home from the office, taking them to nice restaurants, carefully walking on the side next to the curb, chatting politely with the nice couples from their church . . . but sometimes when they were out at the Holmeses', August talked loudly, as loudly as the Holmeses did, about the farm and the cows and the Holmeses' neighbors, some of whom appeared to be thoroughly vulgar, and sometimes arguing violently, without any restraint at all, about state elections. Of course, August and Em had the same upbringing . . . still, what you did with your life after you were grown up should make all the difference.

Certainly Marjory and Millicent were nothing like their Holmes cousins. Now and then Lois turned toward the backseat where the girls sat, and she smiled a warm conspiratorial smile that said, never mind, dears, we will be coming back down this road in a few hours, just a few hours, on our way home again. Just be patient, darlings, try not to mind. And they smiled back at her, their delicate little-girl smiles, shaking their soft brown hair, their pretty brown hair that with only a little encouragement curled in the dearest little ringlets. Lois was always so happy about their hair.

When they got to the Holmeses', August honked the horn loudly before they got out of the car—she hated his doing it—and the Holmeses came tramping out of the farmhouse, shouting as they came. Em and Jim Holmes stood by the gate in the characteristic and, somehow, vulgar Holmes stance, feet planted independently, arms crossed and resting on their stomachs, heads tilted back and a little sidewise, with the friendly but superior air of people who owned a piece of the earth. The Holmes children came running on out to the car, yelling, "Hi, Marge! Hi, Milly! H'are you, Uncle August, Aunt Lois!"

They got into the house in a swirl of laughing and talking; the Holmeses were everywhere. Lois gave her daughters little pats before the Holmes cousins grabbed them; Marjory and Millicent were always a little shy, a little breathless, when they first got there. Em Holmes, a little, brown, restless woman, wanted to know how Lois was, and Lois told her she'd been having her headaches lately, and started to tell her about the new diet her doctor'd put her on, but before she was finished Em was already laughing over a joke Jim was telling August, which, from the last bit of it she caught, was not even very nice.

"Can I help with anything about the dinner?" Lois asked, but Em said firmly no, to sit down and talk with the menfolk; there was very little to do. Sometimes Em, even though she was polite enough, gave Lois the feeling of being in the way. She sat back down and arranged the skirt of her blue dress nicely over her knees. But August, after a moment, wandered out to the kitchen after Em, and soon she heard a low murmur of their voices, and a little later their loud, unrestrained bursts of laughter, sounding very much alike at that distance. It was all right, of course, after all she was his sister; but Lois felt a little lonely, left in the living room to answer politely and uncomfortably to Jim's great rush of talk.

The dinner was good—Em was a very good cook when she bothered—and the Holmeses had wine with it, and so did August but Lois said no thanks, just a glass of water. The talk, so much talk, eddied and flowed about her . . . how *could* these people talk so much . . . lespedeza, egg prices, government subsidies, the county agent is trying to get more people to plant flax, Santa Gertrudis cattle are a cross between the sacred cow of India and the Texas Longhorn, I like the

Polangis stock myself, now you take that land over toward San Angelo, no lime, did you see the piece in the paper about ———, the governor's race should be a good one this time, I really laughed that day at noon when we had the Hillbilly Flour program on KRIS and that flour salesman got up and said he was planning to run. . . .

"I don't know whether it's funny or not," Em said; "he's just a big enough crook to take people in."

Lois wished that Em wouldn't speak so harshly about people; she always tried to teach the girls never to say unkind things about others. "Why, Em," she said, trying hard to make conversation, with difficulty, "I heard him speak over the radio the other day and I thought he sounded like a real good, sincere man."

Em and Jim laughed, and even August, irritatingly, joined in. "I wouldn't bank too much on his goodness, Lois," Em said with a sort of kindness that was harder to bear than if she'd been curt.

The children were getting restless.

"Is it all right to take Marge and Millicent out to look at the kittens now, Aunt Lois?" Ellen Holmes was asking. It was all right; kittens would be very sweet for the girls to look at. "But put your jackets on, girls, you don't want to catch cold," Lois said.

The talk went on; speaking of crooks, de Canales here in the county was one, there was no question about it. Had been mixed up with the McClellan crowd five or six years ago. . . .

The kittens were very sweet. The mother cat looked immensely proud, and the five babies were little and pink and blind, and eager about getting their lunches.

"Why do they have little cords on their stomachs, why *do* they?" Millicent, squatting by the side of the kittens, looked up eagerly at her cousins.

"Oh, for heaven's sakes," Ellen said, "you mean you don't know *that*? It's where they were connected to their mother. You had one yourself."

"We're meeting at Grace's next Wednesday," Lois was telling Em. "Grace has everything so lovely, her husband's so crazy about her, they couldn't have any children, you know, and he gets her just anything she wants. Grace is so cute about it, she always says he just *spoils* her. It's France and Poland next Wednesday, Mrs. Houser is supposed to report on them."

"That ought to be interesting," Em said restlessly, her gaze wandering toward the side porch off the living room, where August and Jim were smoking and talking.

"Oh, we've looked at the cats long enough," Ellen Holmes said impatiently. "Let's go and help Phoenix catch some field rats for them. He doesn't eat them himself, but he loves to catch them. The rats are in the grain stacks in back of the barn, under the bundles, and somebody has to pull out the bundles so that the rats run out, and then Phoenix can grab them."

"Won't they bite?" Marjory said, frightened.

"They might," Ellen said cheerfully. "Not likely to. Phoenix grabs them awfully fast."

They walked down to a small, fenced-in pasture where the grain stacks stood. They crawled through the barbwire fence. "Careful," Ellen said, "you have to decide whether you want to crawl right on the ground under the lower wire or whether you want to go between the first and second wires. I'll hold the wire back a little for you." Phoenix knew what was going to happen, and he waited tense and wriggling while the girls shook the big bundles that made up the stacks, so that any hiding rats would scuttle out into the open: and when they appeared, he grabbed deftly at their necks, and there was a faint, crunching sound. Marjory was still a little afraid, but still it was awfully exciting.

After several had been killed, Ellen said, "It sure is a shame"—she looked at Millicent—"that your cat Andy can't have some of these. It's more than our cats can eat, and they're just going to waste."

"He's never had rat meat, I guess," Millicent said. "Do they really like it?"

"Of course. No cat's really lived until he's had fresh rat meat. Other cats snub him, Mother says."

"I think we'd better take some home to Andy," Millicent said practically, looking at Marjory.

"I don't see just how," Marjory objected.

"We could go into the kitchen and get a paper sack," Ellen said. "Only somebody's likely to notice and ask what we want it for . . . or your socks might do. They're not *very* bloody. I guess four rats would keep till he could get them eaten."

Even August admitted that it was time they were getting home. He was sitting now where he belonged, at the wheel of the car by Lois's side. Her family was pulled together again; their pattern was falling back into shape. They were a firm, united whole, safely in their own car, which would take them decently home to the city. Lois sat beside her husband, beginning to relax, waving cordially at the Holmeses, who were standing around, one of them on the porch, one of them leaning on the gate, two of them in the driveway beside the car, all of them standing in that characteristic Holmes way. But nothing very dreadful had happened, after all. Lois glanced pleasantly at the two pounds of sweet butter in her lap, the firm cabbage and lettuce heads, the basket of fresh eggs piled in the backseat by the girls, and she thought, they're such good people, really.

Nothing dreadful at all had happened, nothing had happened to the girls that a hot bath wouldn't fix. They sat like delicate florists' flowers; their city-bred femininity was still with them. Thinking about them, a thought came back to her that had crossed her mind before but had been interrupted by some Holmes remark.

"And how were the kittens?" Lois asked.

"Oh, they were cute," Millicent said absently, avoiding her glance.

"Girls," Lois said gently, "you shouldn't have taken off your socks, should you? Don't you think you might catch cold on the way home?"

Oddly, neither of the girls answered. They were smiling slightly, their arms were crossed in front of them and their heads tossed back and a little sidewise; and for one awful moment—she couldn't tell why, but they looked just like little Holmeses.

The Last Daughter-in-Law

Mr. and Mrs. Bauer ran the grocery store in Los Altos, Texas. That is, it was mainly a grocery store, but they also had a few bolts of cotton dress goods and shirting, and nails, and aspirin, and things like that. It was a neat, well-stocked store, and their prices were on the whole fair enough; if you didn't like to pay the cent or two more they charged for most things, you were free to drive the twenty miles to Corpus Christi to a supermarket. And while Mr. and Mrs. Bauer's smiles were a trifle professional, their air a little too careful for very easy give-and-take, still they were nice enough; nobody had anything against them, and it was really a good store for such a little town.

Perhaps one reason why the Bauers were not particularly close to most of the people in Los Altos was that they were German and Lutherans. In Los Altos most people were either Baptists or Methodists, aside from the Mexicans, who, of course, were Catholic, and Mrs. Huntingdon, who was a Russelite and believed that following the Judgment Day she was going to live right where she was, except that everything was going to be more perfect and her two little boys who had died would run in and out of the house and call "Mama" to her. Even the Catholics knew that this was pretty fantastic, and that instead they would all be in Heaven together and twang their harps, but people were nice to Mrs. Huntingdon about it, because she'd had lots of sorrow.

Anyway, the Bauers were Lutheran, and on Sundays they drove the twenty miles to church in Corpus Christi, and their only close friends were the few other German Lutherans in the neighborhood. But they were pleasant to everybody, and if sometimes you thought you saw, in back of Mrs. Bauer's smile, a fleeting look of something bordering on distaste when she looked at some of her customers, it was probably just that she had a rather sharp, black, commercial eye. Such times as when Mrs. Jennie Lee Harper, whose family had originated in Virginia by way of Tennessee and were collateral descendents of Robert E. Lee, but who was very careless about paying up her bills, would come teetering in on her high heels and say, "Oh, Mrs. Bauer, I *was* hoping you had saved a very very *very* ripe avocado, just for me!" And you could see it again on her face when the shiftless McClanahans came into town, their six children, all of whose noses needed wiping, traipsing after them.

But whatever the Bauers thought of their neighbors, they kept it to themselves. They were nice about extending credit to the farmers during the winter, and most of them paid up in the spring just as soon as they could. People who wanted credit asked Mr. Bauer about it quietly in the back of the store, but they could feel the gaze of Mrs. Bauer, at the cash register, on them just the same. She was just as soft-spoken and polite as he was, but somehow he was more convincing about it, perhaps only because he was thin and blue-eyed and a little stoop-shouldered, and she was short and square and straight, and her snappy black eye seemed to take in everything at once, from the size of the eggs a farmer was bringing in to sell, to the Mexican five-peso piece the little boys at the jar of jawbreakers were thinking of putting in the slot to see if it would work.

The Bauers had four children—Otto, Henry, Arthur, and Doreen—all of whom in turn entered the first grade in the Los Altos school and finally graduated from high school there. They were nice, well-behaved children, smart enough but not too smart, who played tag and jacks and baseball and basketball with the other children. They didn't know a word of German; when they were little, their parents had still spoken it at home, but when the older ones went to school they were embarrassed about it. And so Mr. and Mrs. Bauer quit speaking it to the children, and eventually they quit speaking it to each other, and by the time the children were grown their parents didn't even have much of an accent left. But they still went to the Lutheran church, and sometimes, when Mrs. Bauer could spare the time from the store, she still made kuchen and potato pancakes.

Things went along pretty well for the Bauers. All the children worked in the store after school and on Saturdays, and the Bauers thought that the oldest one, Otto, and the wife he would someday marry would probably take it over eventually.

Otto, when he got to be seventeen or eighteen, was taking girls out, Jeannie Miller, and Eloise Simmons, and different ones from around town. Mrs. Bauer was usually willing for him to have the car, for he was a reliable boy, and she was always pleasant to his girl-friends, and told their mothers what nice girls they were. But when he was nineteen, and was out of school and working in the store full-time, she grew fond of a young Lutheran lady of German extraction named

Loueen Pohlmeyer, who was the daughter of a well-to-do farmer over toward Corpus Christi. She took to inviting Loueen over for dinner, and inviting her to come home with them from church and spend the day on Sundays, and sometimes inviting her to spend the whole weekend. She often mentioned what a nice, big, healthy, sweet-dispositioned girl Loueen was, the kind who would someday be a real help to a husband, and what pretty blue eyes she had. Otto had never had much occasion to doubt his mother's judgment about anything, and he didn't doubt her judgment in this case, and so eventually he and Loueen got married, and after that both of them helped in the store. But the truth of the matter was that Loueen didn't catch on very fast in the store; she was a good, willing girl, but she couldn't add and she put the tomatoes on the bottom. Mrs. Bauer sighed sometimes, but she said that Loueen was a sweet girl and would improve.

But she didn't improve much, and after about a year Otto said one day, "Mother, Loueen and I have decided that we would like to go into farming." Mrs. Bauer sank into a chair and said, *"Farming!"* in a voice of shock and unbelief. Some people did farm, of course; some of their best friends were farmers. But she couldn't understand why anybody who *could* run a store would voluntarily choose farming as an occupation. However, she and Mr. Bauer talked it over, and he thought maybe it wasn't such a bad idea. After all, Loueen was a farm girl and would be lots more help to Otto on a farm than she was likely to be in the store. Henry was already out of high school, and one of these days he would be getting married, and perhaps he was the one who should take over the store. So Mr. Bauer helped finance the purchase of a farm for Otto and Loueen, who began raising chickens and pigs and cotton, and after a while babies, and both of them lost their white store complexions and grew brown and rosy.

In the meantime, Henry was in Corpus Christi taking a bookkeeping course and forgetting about Myrtle McManus, his mother hoped. All through high school he and Myrtle had spent most of their spare time together, holding hands as sedately as an old married couple. When he came back to the store—and he was needed there, with Otto and Loueen gone, and Arthur and Doreen not yet out of school—Mrs. Bauer took a great fancy to Aleen Spiegelhauer, and began having her over for Sunday dinner. The Spiegelhauers were a tall, pale, thin, blond family of German extraction, who went to the Lutheran church. They were gentle, unenergetic, sweet-natured people, whose women always looked nice and kept a neat house but didn't put up fruit, and whose men ran a gas station over on Highway 10, and were very obliging about checking your tires and wiping your windshield, as long as you weren't in any particular hurry. Aleen, as Mrs. Bauer began remarking frequently, was a nice girl, and just as good-natured as she could be, and would develop more push if she married an up-and-coming young man. Henry, like Otto, had had no occasion to doubt his mother's good sense, and so eventually he and Aleen got married.

But it didn't turn out exactly as Mrs. Bauer had anticipated. Henry worked in the store, and as a result of his bookkeeping course the records were kept much better than ever before. But storekeeping didn't appeal to Aleen; she had no plans for developing any push, for she had married well. She retired to the little house Mr. Bauer had bought for the young couple, and kept it neat and put candles on the dinner table, and served up dainty little meals for Henry when he came home from work, and took care of her nails and complexion the way they advised you to in *Romances of the Stars*. And gradually all of the large Spiegelhauer family came to lean, gently and sweet-naturedly, on the Bauers. When they wanted to transport something, they borrowed the Bauers' trailer, and when they went on trips they borrowed their suitcases, and when they borrowed money the Bauers signed the note.

After a year or so, Henry had a chance at a bookkeeping job for the Standard Oil Company, and told his parents he wanted to take it. The truth of the matter was that Aleen thought it was more genteel to work at a desk than in a grocery store; in the magazine stories she read, husbands came home from the office in the evenings, not home from the meat counter.

"Bookkeeping!" Mrs. Bauer said. "On a *salary*!" It was beyond her comprehension why anyone would want to do such a thing. But she and Mr. Bauer talked it over, and he thought that they might as well make the best of it. After all, there wouldn't be much sense in trying to force Henry into taking over the store if he didn't want to, when there was Arthur, now out of school and in Corpus Christi apprenticed to a butcher.

When Arthur came home, he knew all about meat, and they installed a chicken barbecuing machine, and the roasts were neatly lined with suet and decorated with a bit of parsley. But he wasn't home for long, because pretty soon he was drafted.

So Mr. and Mrs. Bauer managed alone, with the help of their youngest, Doreen. But before Mrs. Bauer had really turned her full attention upon Doreen—for she was now so busy that she didn't really have much attention to give—Doreen got herself engaged to a young man who lived near Corpus Christi, whose name was John Chalupnik, and who was a Czech and a Catholic. Mrs. Bauer was very dismayed at first, but then she thought it over and remembered that one of her grandfathers had been half Czech, and she wasn't sure but what he had been raised a Catholic. Besides, it wasn't as if Doreen was going to run the store. So Doreen took instruction and became a Catholic, and settled down near Corpus Christi to raise little Chalupniks.

So Mr. and Mrs. Bauer were left alone in the store. It was a happy day when Arthur wrote that he was now coming home; but their joy was a nervous joy when they read further and found that he was bringing home a wife, whom he had met when he was stationed near Dallas. He mentioned that she was very pretty, that her name was Esther, and that they would probably be interested to know that her father and mother ran a delicatessen in Dallas. It sounded all right, but somehow Mrs. Bauer felt a vague apprehension.

Esther was very pretty. She was a little, strong, square girl, with dark rosy cheeks and shining black hair and a snapping black eye. Mrs. Bauer said nothing, but then, although she had never been sick in her life, she took to her bed and lay pale and moaning for three weeks. Doreen and Loueen and Aleen brought her chicken soup, but she turned her face to the wall and wept. But finally one morning she got up, and, looking old and thin and shaky, went down to the store.

And there was Esther behind the cash register, giving the customers a cheery, professional greeting, carefully counting out the change, weighing the potatoes with a fast, accurate flip, hustling loitering little boys out so kindly that their own mothers couldn't have objected, and tucking the ripest avocado under the counter for Mrs. Harper. And Arthur whistled behind the meat counter as he decked the lamb chops out in paper frills.

In the evening of the Bauers' lives, Mr. Bauer retired to his garden. It seemed that he had always wanted to raise flowers, and the neat, prosaic lawn gave way to sweet peas and phlox. But Mrs. Bauer sat in a rocking chair in the store and knitted sweaters for the little Chalupniks, and her glance, grown softer now, rested fondly on the bright, black, commercial eye of Esther.

The Cotton Field

Jane's mother called her at six. She got up and put on the clothes she had worn the day before, picking them up from the floor beside the bed where they lay because they were too stiff with dirt and sweat to be put anywhere else.

For a few minutes she couldn't remember why she was not quite happy, and then it came back to her that Kippie had died the day before. The worst part about the death of such as Kippie is that no sympathy is wasted on the mourner; her father had said, "Oh, for God's sake, Jane"; and her mother had said, well, it was too bad, of course, but if Jane never had worse than the death of Kippie to grieve over she would lead a fortunate life, and it wasn't as if she couldn't get another cat, and after all she still had Thomas.

She went down to breakfast, and her little brother looked at her across the breakfast table, silently, with eyes like a catfish's. She didn't think about Kippie, and she ate eggs and cereal, and they tasted good to her.

When she was through, she took the lunch her mother had packed for her and her water jug and Oliver Twist off the kitchen shelf where she had laid him the night before. She went outside and took her dirty gray canvas cotton sack off the barbwire fence and called Thomas.

When she got to the cotton field the sun was well above the horizon but it was still soft and gentle and pale and the air was cool and nice. The cobwebs hanging on the cotton bushes still had dew on them and sparkled in the sun so that they were beautiful laces trimmed with diamonds. She knew, though, that if she looked closely at them they would not be perfect. Sometimes she thought that somewhere in the world there must be a perfect cobweb, where no stitches had been dropped and the pattern had not faltered and no threads had been broken, but it never seemed to be in Texas. Maybe they were more like poor, insubstantial darns where some great frowsy housewife had tried to patch together the ragged cotton plants.

She would look, anyway. She set down Thomas, who was complaining that he was tired of being clutched in her arm, draped around a water jug ("You'd complain more if I'd made you walk," she told him) and her cotton sack and her lunch and Oliver Twist in the row next to the one she'd picked the day before.

She skipped down the row, careful not to leave it for fear she'd never find it again, bending and stooping to look at cobwebs, and then seeing another further on shining in the sun and running to look at it. But it was no use. The spiders were careless, or they forgot, or maybe they really tried very hard and failed.

The sun was getting hotter; the cobwebs were drying off; the diamonds were disappearing. She was a long way from her cotton sack; she couldn't see it anymore. All she could see was an endless world of cotton with far away on the horizon a burned yellow cornfield. She turned and ran back down the row. This year, as in most years, it had rained very little, and the cotton bushes were not much above her shoulder and they looked like hard stiff skeletons, and the cotton looked very bright and almost hid the burned dark leaves. The branches were so hard and sharp that they scratched white marks on her legs as she walked. Last year it had rained more than she could remember it ever raining, and so at the end of July, when picking began, the cotton bushes had been strange, green, fleshy things, with the cotton bolls almost buried in the leaves. The bushes had been over her head—of course she was a little shorter then, too—and the weeds had flourished in the middles. She felt old and wise, having a memory of another year . . . a rainy year, last year.

She stepped carefully along the row, even when she ran, and without thinking about it she looked hard at each spot before she put her foot down on it, because of rattlesnakes, although the bad time for them was in spring. Twice a stalk of striped careless-weed lay across her path and she stopped with a jerk, and when at last a harmless baby of a chicken snake did slide from under a bush she gave a little scream and then laughed, and the sounds were small and flat in the stillness. No bird sang, no insect whirred, no breeze rustled the dry leaves, and the little snake went on its way, probably, she thought, to the grocery or the hairdresser's, quickly and in silence. Nothing was alive, nothing moved, but her and the little snake and the sun.

When she got back to her sack she saw that Thomas had quite given up and was stretched out, limp and unconscious and deafened and made senseless by the sun. "It's not yet that hot," she told him, but he never stirred. She put the strap over her head, over her left shoulder and across her to the right, so that the mouth of the cotton sack swung open under her right hand. She began to pick.

Now and then she stopped for a moment to push the plastered strands of her hair out of her face. She glanced at the sun, still well to the east of her, and tried to guess the time. Once she saw great dark birds swinging slowly across the face of the sun, and they seemed far, far up.

Sometime, she thought, she would pick as much cotton in a day as Esther Robinson. She did not like Esther Robinson. When school started in September Esther would say carelessly, but loud enough for everyone to hear, that she had picked two hundred pounds a day again. Maybe she would have picked even more this year. She would say, "How much did you pick, Jane?"

She thought of Kippie again. She rather wished it had been Thomas, and then she hurt inside for having thought anything so cruel about Thomas, after he had let her bring him to the cotton field and now lay sleeping, his old pink mouth a little open because of the heat, in the poor shade of a cotton bush. Her father had taken Kippie's little gray body to the east field.

She looked at the sun again and saw that the great black birds were buzzards and that they were circling far lower now, in slow, swaying circles.

There was no reason why she could not pick two hundred pounds in a day if Esther Robinson could. She bent her back, although it was beginning to get tired, down lower to the cotton, and snatched furiously at the bolls, paying no attention when she scratched her hands, poking the cotton swiftly into the sack, not bothering now if occasionally the boll came with the cotton, ignoring moths and caterpillars and odd little green bugs. The sun seemed to be coming closer and closer toward her, and she could not tell whether it was the sun or her head that was throbbing, and she felt the back of her neck and her arms browning like a roast in the oven.

She straightened up at last and lifted her bag off the ground, but she couldn't guess how many pounds were in it. Quite a few, maybe. She looked at the sun and decided that it was almost noon. She walked back down the row to where she had begun—it was a shorter way than it had seemed—and drank thirstily and ate sandwiches, chewing slowly, with her eyes looking somewhere on the ground in front of her, but at nothing in particular, and with nothing in particular in her mind except a vague feeling that her back hurt. She shook the dirt out of her shoes and put them on again; she wiped her face the best she could with her handkerchief. She took out Oliver Twist and, laying him in the shade, began to read.

The sun climbed and the field seemed to take on a startled bluish tinge and the heat came down and was all around her. The hot white balls of clouds in the sky and the hot white balls in the cotton field were alike and confused, and no one could have said which was which. The sun came closer and closer and it made a blare like drums and cymbals and loud piercing horns.

She laid her face against the hot earth and put one arm around Thomas and sobbed—because Kippie was dead, and Oliver Twist was inescapably imprisoned in a book and through all eternity would have to go hungry for a dish of gruel in Chapter 6, and she would never, never be able to pick two hundred pounds of cotton in a day—but silently, for the sun was sound, and from directly above her was bellowing down at her in vast crescendos.

The School Bus

It was the year that Jane quit walking the mile down the road to school every day and began riding a school bus instead. This happened because the school district she lived in annexed the Rancho Casa Blanca district. The two teachers who had taught at the Rancho went away, and the little schoolhouse was boarded up, its windows looking blind the way everybody's windows did late in August when the radio said that a hurricane was sweeping up the Gulf of Mexico.

So that fall a great orange school bus went trundling out down the dusty road every day ten or fifteen miles to the Rancho country and brought in the children, giggling and squirming and screaming, and yet already tired when they got to school at eight-forty-five, because most of them had walked a long way at daybreak to get to the bus line.

"There's no reason," Jane's mother had said, a week or so before school opened, "why, if there's room enough, Jane shouldn't ride in with the school bus, too, even if they did get it for the Rancho children." So Jane's father, who was on the school board, asked the superintendent, who was feeling good with the new importance of being superintendent to two school districts instead of one; and he said sure, Jane could ride on the school bus if she wanted. Of course she'd have to be ready in the mornings and out on the right-hand side of the road; the school bus didn't wait on anyone. He said that if many children had lived, like Jane, only a mile or so from school in the Rancho direction there wouldn't have been room, but since there was just Jane it would be all right.

Jane felt a little funny about riding on the school bus. She didn't know any of the people from the Rancho country, but her father and her older brother, Edward, sometimes mentioned them, and last year there had been a shooting out there that had even got into the Corpus Christi *Caller-Times*. She knew that some of them didn't want to ride the school bus in to the bigger school; her father said several of the families had

been right ornery about it, but enough of them had finally come around so that the vote had carried. Her father said that the Rancho people were mostly pretty
trashy and that some of the families had lice and sore-
eyes and things like that, and so it would probably be
best for her not to hang herself around their necks, as
he put it.

She had seen where they came from. Sometimes in
the early summer her father would say on a Sunday
afternoon, "Mom, would you like to drive out west
and look at the crops?" And Jane and her mother
would tie something around their heads, because of the
strong wind that always blew off the gulf, and go driving in the car out to the Rancho country, going slow
and staring out at other people's cows and gazing criti-
cally down the pivoting rows of other people's cotton,
and craning curiously at the pastures of Rhodes grass,
because the seed had come from Africa, and going
faster past the parts that were just miles and miles of
prairie.

Jane had seen the Rancho country then. The great
spread-eagle electric poles stopped when you got out
there, and the dirt road got narrower and more crooked,
and the scattered houses got smaller and smaller and
were really just little boxes, built with the boards going up and down. Great families of thin noisy children
spilled out of them, and gray ragged clothes flapped on

the clotheslines beside them. Sometimes they passed a ranch boss's house, and it was a little better and might even be painted and have curtains, and sometimes they passed a whole row of Mexican houses, with just open places for doors and banty chickens wandering in and out, and roofs patched with cans spread out and nailed down. Sometimes great pieces of dried goat meat, almost black with flies, and bunches of drying peppers and gourds would be hanging by the door. And in the dirt yards would be fires and pots where the beans were cooking, and old, old Mexican women, bent over and with black shawls over their heads, would be watching and stirring slowly. And the thin hound dogs that stood around by the doorway would be Mexican dogs—you could tell.

Sometimes they drove past smelly, miry corrals, with thin swaybacked cows standing around in them, and the great wind blew the smell right into the car. Sometimes they passed women working in the fields, even though it was Sunday, and sometimes they passed men along the road who were great and hairy and freckled and red-faced and who seemed always to be shouting as they drove by, and who had bowlegs and wore great boots and spurs. And Jane looked, and saw that the thin horses' sides were scarred and cut.

When they got home, her father would say, "Well, Mom, I don't know that I saw any cotton any prettier than ours on the east twenty." And her mother would say yes, she hadn't realized how good it was.

The cotton season was short that summer, and so the beginning of school came early. In the mornings Jane walked down the big front steps and the weedy flagstone walk and through the salt cedar trees to the road to wait for the bus, feeling conscious of her new school shoes and her new tablet and her long pencils. Somehow, it was painful to stand there watching the great orange bus that at first was just a little orange speck far across the flat prairie and then grew bigger and bigger, watching and knowing that it would stop for her and that the big door would open for her and that she would step up into it with dozens of eyes looking just at her.

She noticed, the first days, that the shrill laughing and talking stopped when she got in. At first nobody said anything at all, and then later someone would occasionally say something to her that was neither friendly nor unfriendly, some statement that left her uncomfortable and, somehow, apologetic. Once a thin little girl whose name was Bessie looked at Jane's fresh starched dress and said sharply, "Your mama washed that dress yesterday. I seen it on the line yesterday afternoon."

She was afraid of them, and it was days before she looked at them enough to see what they looked like, and then she saw that most of them were freckled fair children with dirt under their fingernails and streaky yellow hair that had been cut at home with jags and dips in it, with bare tough feet and stocky, pasty-fleshed, unclean arms and legs with thick blond hairs on them. Their teeth were like old men's, and sometimes they had great ugly scabs on their faces, and Jane shrank from them a little.

They usually sat toward the front, and in back of them in a little huddled knot sat the Mexican children, small, shrinking, afraid. They looked cold, even though it was still hot in September; Jane would look at them sometimes and be surprised to see that their dark unwashed skins had the look of gooseflesh about them. They sat very still, and their faces never seemed to change, but their black eyes, looking out from the ancient little faces with an intense, opaque, Indian look, followed what the blond children did, watched them talk together, watched them pinch each other and slap each other, watched them shout and scuffle and laugh uproariously.

And then one afternoon, going home, a little girl turned on Jane and said, "I guess you make good grades."

"Of course she does, her father's on the school board," the girl across the aisle said. Jane looked at them and tried to smile, but nobody smiled back, and she saw that their faces were suddenly angry and that their pale mouths were hard.

The thin little girl named Bessie, who was sitting beside her, scornfully flipped the edge of Jane's skirt, bright beside all the faded ones, and cried, "It's a Mexican dress, with them bright checks! I bet your mama got it at Garcia's!"

Jane looked from one to another and saw that more and more of the faces were turning to her. The boys, who were sitting together, were beginning to stop their own intimate laughing and were turning, leaning forward, interested, eager, their pasty faces more alive than usual. And the little knot of strange grave black eyes was looking toward her, too, silently watching. The driver's back was big, solid, blue denim, uninterested.

"Did you ever pick cotton?" someone shouted. "I bet anything you never picked cotton at all." "*I wouldn't ride a school bus if I lived just a mile from town, I walk that much just to get to the school bus,*" several of them seemed to be saying. Their voices were louder and louder, they were crowding toward her, and their freckled, scabbed faces were pushing closer and closer to hers, and the smell of them pressed in upon her. The driver's back shifted a little in the seat; skillfully he steered the bus, following the deep ruts in the road worn since the last rain. *"You're no better than anybody else,"* everybody in the bus seemed to be shouting at her. *"Did you ever milk a cow? . . . Did you ever pick cotton?"*

The bus was stopping; they were even with her house. She ran, the voices staying in her ears so that she did not know whether they had stopped or not. As she grabbed her lunch basket and books together more firmly, she looked back at the bus and saw, surprised, that the children were not looking at her anymore and that they had stopped shouting. They were looking through the salt cedars up the incline at the big white house, standing in the shady yard where the splashy pink and white oleanders and the ragged fig trees grew, at the bright white washing fluttering on the line and the plump Leghorn hens singing in the backyard, and at the great lawn of Bermuda pasture to the west of the house, where the fat cows were grazing and the calves were playing.

I Cannot
Tell a Lie,
Exactly

"*Mother,*" says Jimmie tentatively, but she does not hear him. All of the family have left the dinner table except her, but she has poured herself a second cup of tea and is sitting there amid the wreckage of the meal reading the morning paper. She looks tired but cheerful, for just as Harry Truman's mother wrote of earning, by her hard pioneer-woman's days, the right to do fancywork in the evenings, so Julia has earned the right to read the morning paper. She has met the problems of the day, one by one, and conquered them, and their dissevered heads are strewn down the path of the hours that lie behind her. It is seven-thirty, and all she has yet to do is to put the dishes in the dishwasher and clean up the kitchen and feed the cats and check Bruce's arithmetic homework. She almost has it made.

"Mother," says Jimmie more urgently, for he has something to tell her that, it now seems to him, he should perhaps have mentioned a week or two ago. He is nine, and he has not yet had much experience at breaking things gently.

"Yes," she answers, without looking up. Something in the paper strikes her as funny, and there is a slight smile on her face.

"Mother," he repeats, "I need a white wig."

"Whatever for?" she asks mildly, her eyes still on the paper.

"I'm going to be George Washington in a play."

"That's nice," she says.

"But I need this white wig," he says.

"When is the play going to be?" she asks.

"Tomorrow morning," he says, bracing himself.

"*Tomorrow morning?*" she cries.

"For the whole school," he says humbly, offering it in consolation.

She flings the paper from her and exclaims, "You should have *told* me," but there is no time to waste in recriminations. She has instantly mobilized into a mother, the engines racing, the smokestacks billowing, and the gun turrets swung into place.

"Roger!" she calls as she flies down the stairs, but he does not hear her. Roger has had a hard day, and he has earned the right to watch television; he is stretched out on the couch, a faint smile on his face. "Roger," she cries, planting herself in front of him, "you must go this instant to the drugstore for a roll of surgical cotton!"

"Are you out of your mind?" he inquires with only a mild and routine hostility, craning his neck to see the screen around her.

"Jimmie has to be George Washington tomorrow morning, and he needs a wig!"

"Well, don't make a scene about it," he says. "Surely we have a wig around here."

"Don't be absurd!" she snaps. But he is rummaging in a closet.

"There!" he says triumphantly, producing it.

Bruce has finished his arithmetic and has joined Julia and Jimmie, and three pairs of eyes now look at Roger with stony contempt, for, his mind on his television program, he has grasped "wig," but not "George Washington."

"Roger," says Julia in a voice of fire and ice, "Jimmie cannot be the Father of his Country in a Beatle wig, and that's final. Now will you *please* go to the drugstore?"

Cowed, he puts on his coat, but at the door he

turns around. "What's wrong with the cotton batting that goes around the Christmas tree?"

He has redeemed himself; they all look at him with new respect. It is brought down from the attic. It will not only do, but do better, for it comes in a large piece. Julia does say that George Washington may look as if he could stand a shampoo (the batting has survived a number of Christmases), but she concedes that it will serve nicely. She already has her scissors into Jimmie's last summer's cap, exploring for the threads that hold the visor on, for a base is needed for the wig.

"Surely," exclaims Roger, "you're not going to tear up his perfectly good cap?"

"It's too small for him," she says.

"If it's too small to be a cap, how come it's big enough to be a wig?" he asks, for her brazen liberties with the truth madden him sometimes.

"It *will* be too small by summer," she says calmly. It is too late to argue; she has already reduced it to a mere skullcap, and has clapped it onto Jimmie's head and is draping the batting over it in a first approximation. Roger abandons logic and grabs at the other side; they twitch it in the direction of a pigtail down the back. "Not bad . . . yes, more this way . . . no, farther back from the forehead," they murmur to each other.

Jimmie, patiently posing, suddenly realizes what they are doing.

"You're not going to put a pigtail on it," he wails. "George Washington didn't *have* one!"

Their hands stop in midair. Surely, in those silhouettes of George and Martha . . .

"No, he didn't, he really didn't," cries Bruce; he runs to his room, and they hear the sounds of things being thrown out of drawers, and he comes back with a color print of Savage's portrait of the Washington family, which he once selected on a class trip to an art gallery, and a last year's calendar with Stuart's Washington on the cover. It is true; the hair is ear-length and fluffy, and, so far as can be seen, there is no pigtail.

Julia sits down with needle and thread and begins on the forehead, which is high and plain, and sews awhile, and puts it back on Jimmie's head and studies the effect, and sews some more. Roger thinks she is doing it wrong. He watches her, his fingers twitching a little, the saliva tending to accumulate in his mouth; it is like watching someone untangle string. Finally he can stand it no more, and he exclaims that she is ruining it. She asks whether he thinks he can do better, and he says that he certainly can and will. The needle comes unthreaded in the transfer, and so he begins by holding it aloft and ramming the thread at it, his thumb and forefinger racing it along toward the needle like firemen carrying a hose; they miss, back up, and charge again. Bruce is doubled over with laughter, for he has never seen his father try to thread a needle before. But Jimmie, his usual tact with his parents forsaking him, cries in alarm, "Mother, don't you *dare* let Daddy make my wig!" Julia giggles; she has a slight mean streak in her, and she enjoys this thoroughly. Roger, stung, lays down the wig and the needle and thread without a word and sulks. It is unfair; after all, it was he, as they had all freely conceded at the time, who, when a Dalmatian foxhound costume was involved, had supervised the size and arrangement of the brown felt spots and narrowly saved it from being an Irish setter.

Julia, sewing busily, has a disturbing thought. What *else* does Jimmie need for his costume? But it seems there is no problem. He is to wear a white shirt (they have already, at school, made paper lace cuffs for it) and long dark pants, with white knee socks pulled over to produce knee breeches, and they have made buckles to decorate his shoes. Only the wig is needed.

Bruce says, "When are you going to check my arithmetic, Mother?" and as he waves his paper in the air a glimpse of dense and close-knit long division floats by. She is not, if the truth were told, particularly fast at long division, and she doesn't have time. "You just check it yourself," she tells him. "Multiply it back."

"Goll-ee," he laments. "That'll take me ages. Dad, won't you check my arithmetic?"

"Multiply it back," he says callously; he cannot bear to take his eyes off the wig; he is waiting, just waiting, to see what she plans to do with all that batting that is bunching up behind the ears. Julia knows exactly what he is waiting for, and she is ceaselessly perfecting the front and sides; occasionally her hands move toward the back as if to start on it, and hesitate and dart away again. She is tantalizing him; and, besides, she hasn't yet figured out how to tackle the area behind the ears.

But something distracts Roger. "Jimmie," he says, "is this a *speaking* part?"

"Sure," says Jimmie, and Roger and Julia look at him with a new worry in their eyes. Does he know his lines?

"Sure," repeats Jimmie, and he begins, in a high, stilted voice, "Martha, tomorrow I must leave by stagecoach for Philadelphia, in order to attend the First Continental Congress. I am delighted that John Adams and Thomas Jefferson will also be able to attend, for . . ."

"Goll-ee," says Bruce. "How does anybody expect anybody to multiply with a racket like that going on?"

Jimmie is thinking, as he has often thought before, that his parents always worry about the wrong things. He knows his part. But there is something else that he really should tell them about. "Mother," he says gently, but she pays no attention. "Mother," he says more loudly, and biting off a thread she looks up. "You know I'm supposed to get my Bear badge in Cub Scouts tomorrow night?"

"Yes," she says abstractedly. She is racing against time, for nine o'clock is Jimmie's bedtime, and all the trying and fitting should be done by then.

"The thing is," Jimmie says, groping for the best way of putting it, "I told them I would have all my Bear achievements done by the pack meeting tomorrow night, and they've got my name down and ordered the badge for me, and they're going to announce it to the whole pack, but there's still one achievement I haven't done."

"Well," says Julia soothingly, "is it learning your state flower, or another kind of knot, or something like that? You've still got about twenty minutes till bedtime, so maybe you can do your achievement right now."

"The trouble is," says Jimmie, "this achievement is a Family Night."

Julia and Roger freeze. "What," they cry, almost together, "is a Family Night?" Bruce, lying on the floor multiplying, senses crisis and looks up, his lips still moving.

"Well," says Jimmie meekly, and he brings his Cub Scout book out from behind his back, "it says here: 'You've made a lot of things as a Cub Scout, but did your family ever spend an evening making things together? Plan and hold a family handicraft night, when you and your family will make things together.' "

"Do you mean to say," roars Roger, "that you have committed us to having done this thing by tomorrow evening's meeting? There's no *time*!"

Jimmie stands there twisting his Cub Scout book in his hands and looking miserable, and his eyes moisten slightly. He is a competent little boy, but just lately his life has been burdened with more responsibilities than he can manage.

Julia drops her hands, letting the wig fall into her lap, and lays her head back and shuts her eyes. She has dramatic talent, and she is unreeling a scene in her head. The photography is amateur, and the direction is rough in spots, but the thing is nonetheless poignant. Fifty Cub Scouts and close to a hundred parents are assembled in the Scout hall. The lights are turned low, with only a spotlight playing on the cubmaster, who stands there, remote and official in his uniform, and calls out names. As he calls Jimmie's name, he holds the Bear badge ready in his left hand and his right hand is already reaching out for the congratulatory handshake. "Have you, James Harrison, completed all the achievements and requirements for this Bear badge?" he intones. Jimmie, in his blue uniform and with his little Scout cap tilted at the regulation angle, has marched bravely forth into the circle of light, and, looking very small and forlorn, he says, "No, sir. I cannot tell a lie. My family hasn't ever made anything together." There is a sensation in the hall.

But suddenly Julia's eyes fly open and she shouts, "We're *doing* it! This *is* Family Night! We're spending an evening making something together!"

They all brighten a little, considering it hopefully; still, there are objections. "I don't know whether we're really doing it *together*," says Bruce practically. "*I'm* doing homework." But she is indomitable. "You have played a vital part," she says impressively. "*You* found the pictures of George Washington and kept us from putting a pigtail down the back."

"Well, we're *holding* a Family Night, but I don't know whether we exactly *planned* it," says Jimmie, who is an honorable Cub Scout.

But Roger is a man who can be relied upon when the chips are down. "Not far ahead, no," he says judiciously. "I don't feel we can be given high marks on the planning end of it. Still, there was unquestionably *some* planning. *You* planned to have a wig, and your mother planned to make it of surgical cotton, and I planned to make it of Christmas tree batting."

Jimmie subsides contentedly. Julia signs her name in Jimmie's book to "Family Night—Achievement 10," and her conscience hardly quivers at all.

Bedtime has come. The wig is finished, and they circle around Jimmie, studying it from this angle and that, as he admires himself in the mirror. His little round face under the white wig looks pink and innocent, and, he thinks, *exactly* like George Washington.

"Well," says Julia at last, "is there any chance you'll be wearing one of those three-cornered hats?"

Oh, yes, Jimmie tells her; the hats are already made.

They all beam. Under a three-cornered hat, they agree, the wig will look stupendous.

The boys are asleep at last, and Julia, finishing tidying the kitchen, looks up to see Roger in the doorway, the wig, too small for him, sitting crookedly on top of his head.

"Coming, Martha?" he says, and arm in arm they go off to bed.

Las Altas

THE PETERSON SITUATION

$\mathcal{M}$rs. $\mathcal{P}$eterson was a droopy little woman who came one summer to live in Las Altas, her husband being an oil well gauger who had been transferred to the Santa Alicia oil field, some twenty miles from Las Altas. In the fall Mrs. Peterson got a job teaching Spanish in the high school. No one felt greatly drawn to her, and she was not an inspiring teacher, but everybody credited her with being good as gold, as people do to a quiet little woman with a sad face and a red nose; and in this case it was no doubt perfectly true.

Mr. Peterson came to town on weekends. Unfortunately, it soon appeared that he spent his weekends getting drunk, and occasionally beating up Mrs. Peterson as well. Mrs. Sue Brattlesby, who lived close to the Petersons, was the first to perceive this, and she told the Farm Bureau gin manager's wife, Mrs. Hitchcock, after which the entire American Legion Auxiliary knew about it.

Before long, there was a substantial public demand that something be done, because after all, something like that going on right in town and a member of the faculty and all, was certainly a scandal and not a good influence on the growing youth of Las Altas. In numerous conversations around town it came to be agreed that the best course would be to offer Mrs. Peterson (poor thing, it wasn't her fault) two alternatives: either Mr. Peterson should stay away weekends and get drunk elsewhere, or she should resign from her schoolteaching job. All of this was brought to the attention of the various members of the school board, and before long Mr. Habbersett, the president of the board, felt required to call a meeting to discuss the problem.

One of the school board members was Mr. Morgenroth, a square little old farmer with white hair and a strong jaw, who had been educated for the Methodist ministry. The evening of the school board meeting, Mr. Morgenroth, ordinarily the mildest of men, slammed things around as he finished his chores and hurried through his supper so as to get down to the school-house on time. Mrs. Morgenroth and the children, sensing that he was in a mood to Take a Stand, scurried around and fetched his coat and hat and spectacles, and backed out the car for him, and stood out of his way.

The school board assembled, and the meeting was opened. The situation was gone over in some detail, with members contributing that they wanted to do what was fair to everybody concerned; that it was a sad case; that oil field workers were generally a hard lot; that Mrs. Peterson was a good little woman; but that the only solution was the one more or less agreed upon by the community—either he stay away or she resign. Mr. Morgenroth didn't say anything until the discussion had pretty well exhausted itself, and then he said that there was a good deal in what everybody had said but that what God hath joined together let no man put asunder. He took his hat and got up. The other members said, Well . . . and somehow the meeting disintegrated, and everybody went home in a tentative sort of way. The members were evasive when they reached home and their wives asked what the board had done about the Peterson Situation.

Mrs. Peterson kept on teaching high-school Spanish, and Mr. Peterson continued to come on weekends, and to beat Mrs. Peterson up, occasionally. Mrs. Peterson, for her part, went out to the Morgenroth farm (for the story had eventually got around), and she fell on Mr. Morgenroth's neck, he looking very stiff and nervous, and said emotionally, with her nose redder than ever, how could she ever thank him for all he had done for her.

Mathilda Maynard and Henry Wagner

While people were pretty upset for a while about the Petersons, still the Petersons were not really local people, and anyway after a year or so they moved on, as oil field people do. But year in, year out, if the citizens of Las Altas, a calm set of people who voted dry on their local option regularly, wanted their blood pressures raised, they could just turn their thoughts to Mathilda Maynard and Henry Wagner.

Both Mathilda and Henry came from perfectly good old Las Altas families. The Wagners owned a section and a half of land on the Benavides road, and were always honest as daylight and good farmers, their only fault being a tendency to hold a grudge. The Maynards owned rent houses in town, and always kept them in pretty good shape, and collected the rent promptly; the women were excellent housekeepers and good bread bakers, although known to be set in their ways.

By this time Mathilda and Henry were the only

members left of their immediate families, the old folks having passed on, Mathilda being an only child, and Henry's brothers and sisters having moved away. Henry was left running the Wagner farm, and was a good farmer, and every year raised some of the prettiest cotton in the county. Mathilda managed her rent houses, and lived on in the big old Maynard house across from the Hitchcocks'. She baked bread, which was always popular at Ladies' Aid sales, and she kept her lawn and flowerbeds as neat as a pin, and she watered her potted plants, and afternoons she sat and rocked on her shady gallery (as a big porch running all around the front and side of the house is called in Las Altas), and did her mending.

The only thing against Mathilda and Henry was that they'd been going together for the last twenty-five years, and they just hadn't gotten married. They went visiting together, and sometimes they went to church together, and occasionally they went in to Corpus Christi to shop together, and once in a while they went to funerals together. All that, so far as it went, was all right; however, Mrs. Hitchcock said that sometimes Henry's pickup, which he drove in from the farm, would sit in front of the Maynard house all night. And once when Mathilda's aunt stopped by, there was Mathilda rocking on her gallery and mending a pair of khaki pants, just as pretty as you please.

This situation bothered Las Altas considerably, even though it was generally understood how it had come about. The fact of the matter was that Mathilda and Henry had been going together only a few years when his brother, who had a real good seed business in Houston, asked him to come in with him as a partner. So Henry asked Mathilda to marry him, and they'd sell their property and move to Houston, and live in style and see a movie whenever they wanted.

Mathilda said *What*, leave Los Altas where she'd been born and raised and owned her own home and three rent houses besides, and where her mama and papa were laid to their eternal rest? Anyway, she had heard that Houston was kinda swampy, and the water there hadn't any taste to it. She dusted off her parents' pictures, and went out to the kitchen to put her bread to rise.

Henry said This, then, was good-bye, and Mathilda said All right, good-bye.

He said good-bye several times more, but he never went. He stayed right there in Las Altas, and farmed his section and a half, although he was grumpy ever afterward. And out of pure spite he never proposed again.

THE CANNON FAMILY

The water in Las Altas has a phenomenally low bacteria count, and tastes as though it would be good for a torpid liver. The taste is presumably compounded of salt, iodine, sulfur, and various other minerals in which the Gulf Coast of Texas is rich; and the absence of bacteria indicates that bacteria have more sense than commonly given credit for. One day it will occur to some thoughtful and enterprising Las Altan to found a spa and bottling works, and he will get rich; in the meantime the natives toss the stuff down without giving it a second thought, retain their teeth to an ancient age, and come back from journeys with word that water other places has no taste to it.

One time a family named Cannon moved to Las Altas from some place in Arkansas, Mr. Cannon being sent there as section boss for the Katy Railroad (which derives its name from the circumstance that Missouri generally gets overlooked in the combination of Missouri, Kansas, and Texas). The Cannons, who, being from Arkansas, were bound to be a little at a disadvantage—nobody is quite so kindly condescending toward an Arkansan as a Texan—were soon conceded to be probably good people in their way, but common. The brown section boss's house proceeded to spill over with an unreckonable number of lanky-haired, only medium-clean little Cannons, and a Cannon appeared in each of the eleven grades of the Las Altas school.

Aside from sheer force of numbers, there was only one thing about the Cannons that really gave Las Altas pause. The young Cannons reported to their fellows in the first through eleventh grades, which fellows reported at home, that the Cannons had to put salt in the Las Altas water, because it didn't have any taste without.

Sober, Exper., Work Guar.

I was just barely making it, with the payments coming around regular on the mortgage, and the car, and the television, and the washing machine, and the encyclopedia, and the kids in parochial school and needing as many shoes as if they was centipedes, and then the dentist said braces.

"Braces!" I yelled when Genevieve told me. "These dentists nowadays got the idea that nobody can even grow their own choppers without their installing a headful of hardware!" But Genevieve's face was clouding up for rain, and I could see there wasn't going to be any use arguing.

There was only one thing to do. Night work. And I can tell you it's no particular fun to plaster all day for Brown Bros. Construction and come home at five and grab dinner and dash off to fix somebody's lousy plaster cracks all evening and knock off in time to get some sleep so you can do the same thing all over again.

I put a ad in the Arlington, Virginia, *Sun*. I live in Arlington—you know, right across the Potomac River from Washington, D.C.—and I figured on getting some job close to home. The ad said:

> Plastering, eves. Free estimate.
> No job too small.
> Sober, exper., work guar.
> JA 8-9643.

I got a few calls, jokers who would get me to come and make a estimate, and then I'd never hear from them again. Probably decided to do it themselves. This do-it-yourself business has really got out a hand in the suburbs. One job I could of had was way the hell out in Fairfax County, take me a hour to get there and a hour to get back. It was no good for making a few bucks in the evenings.

Finally I got this call from a Mr. Ferguson. I went out and made the estimate—they was redoing the kitchen and one whole wall needed replastering. It was one of those big old handsome frame houses set in the middle of a couple of acres of lawn and trees that you still see a few of in the suburbs. Most of them have been tore down to make room for eight or ten split-levels. Mr. Ferguson had a English accent. I never did decide whether that accent was phony or not; it seemed to me he sometimes sounded more English than others. His wife was a plain American, though. A very plain American—a thin little thing with her hair skinned back in a ponytail. As far as looks goes, she wasn't in the same class with Genevieve, although I later decided she was real nice.

I give Ferguson the estimate, and he didn't give me any of this well-we'll-have-to-think-it-over business. He looked me in the eye and said, "Too high." It was maybe a mite high, but it wasn't all that high. Anyway, we batted the thing backwards and forth a while, and finally I come down a little, and we made the deal. But first he asked me, "What did you mean in your ad about 'work guaranteed'?"

"I guarantee my plastering isn't going to crack," I said.

"And what if it *does* crack?" he asked.

"I come back and fix it free," I said, not too enthusiastic. I wasn't sure I liked this guy's attitude, but, still, I needed the work.

I started knocking out the old plaster the next evening. It was plain to see that Ferguson wasn't going to be off somewhere reading a pile of good books while I worked on his plaster. He was right there in back of my left shoulder, in Oxford gray flannel, complete with collar and tie, choking a little on plaster dust but handing out advice free. While I nailed on a new lath, Ferguson was saying, "Another nail or two right here, I think, Mr. Cromwell—we want everything tight and shipshape, don't we?" When I laid on the brown coat, Ferguson, so help me, first asked me what it *was* and then told me how I ought to square it off better in the corners. But it was while I was getting the white coat ready that I nearly lost control. You know how fresh plaster looks—snow-white, and it mixes up in peaks and swirls and looks like it was all ready to frost a cake. Ferguson was leaning over the tub of it saying, "Don't you think perhaps you've put in just a *drop* too much water, Mr. Cromwell?" and I was leaning over the other side of the tub, bringing up a trowelful of that beautiful white stuff, and that trowel was about one foot from Ferguson's face—and, well, he just never knew how close he come. The Fergusons had these two little boys, I guess about seven and nine, and while Ferguson followed me around, they followed *him* around. We was a regular procession. They was learning how to meddle at Daddy's knee, and he was qualified to teach it—beginners, intermediate, and advanced. They never said a word; they was just quiet and big-eyed, looking on admiringly while Daddy told me how to plaster.

And yet in spite of it all I couldn't help but like Ferguson. For instance, a couple of nights after I started, Ferguson wandered in with a bottle of whiskey and was getting out some ice, and he turned to me and said, "Would you care for a drink, Mr. Cromwell?" I said, "No, thanks," but I hesitated so long before I said it that he looked at me sharp and said, "Are you sure, Mr. Cromwell?"

"Yes, I'm sure," I said. "I don't know whether you've ever had any experience with your wife leaving you, Mr. Ferguson, but it's a messy and inconvenient business. I will not deny that Genevieve had some justification at the time, but she has since taken a extreme position and says if she ever so much as smells whiskey on my breath she'll leave me again."

"Oh," said Ferguson, and he stoppered the bottle and put the ice away—none for him either. He was a gentleman all the way through. He stood there, with his arms folded, watching me work for a while, and then he said,

"How does Mrs. Cromwell feel about beer on your breath, Mr. Cromwell?"

"Beer she'll tolerate, if it ain't too steady," I said, and he got us a bottle apiece.

But the nicest thing about Ferguson was that he appreciated good work. When I finished the kitchen wall, he stood there and studied it, and finally he said, "Mr. Cromwell, you are not a plasterer, you are an artist. That is a beautiful wall, and I wish to congratulate you." He paid up, and then he said, "Mr. Cromwell, let us discuss the dining room," which had a few cracks, and we made a deal on that.

The evening I started the dining room I come in and saw Mrs. Ferguson and I got a shock. You never seen a worse sight in your life. She was up on a ladder painting the kitchen, and she had on one of Ferguson's old white shirts with the sleeves hacked off any which way, and a pair of his old gray flannel pants slashed off at the bottoms and taken up around the waist with about six giant safety pins, and a dishtowel tied around her head. I've never seen Genevieve look like that, and I never expect to. But she called out cheerful from the top of the ladder, "Hello, Mr. Cromwell," and she give me her sweet, sunny smile shining through the paint spots.

It upset me to see her painting. If there's one thing I can't stand, it's people messing up nice plastering with sloppy amateur painting. But I needn't have worried. Her work was good. She understood the importance of sealer, and she kept her brush or roller, whichever she was using at the time, moving in the same direction, and she had a sharp eye for drips.

So we settled into a regular routine. I went, one room at a time, through the whole first floor of that big old house, and Mrs. Ferguson worked behind me, a room at a time. Ferguson would get home about six-thirty, all well-pressed suit and briefcase, and lay down his *Washington Post* and his *Wall Street Journal* and his umbrella and take up the burden of supervising. He was terrible overworked now, with two of us to look after. He'd say to her, "My love, I believe your wood-work enamel is getting a trifle too thick—shall we add just a touch of paint thinner?" And he'd say to me, flattening his head against the wall until the under ear began to turn purple, and rolling his eyes practically out of their sockets, "There is not a *ridge* where the crack was, Mr. Cromwell, I wouldn't say a *ridge,* but there is definitely a *ripple.*"

I always kind of enjoyed the hour or so she and I would work along together before he got home in the evenings. We was companionable. Sometimes we'd work a long time without saying anything, but other times we'd talk. Once I said to her, "You know, Mrs. Ferguson, a lot of women wouldn't do what you do. They wouldn't think it was women's work."

She put her head back and laughed, and she was really sort of pretty when she laughed like that, paint spots and all. "Mr. Cromwell," she said, "as far as I'm concerned there isn't really any men's work and women's work. There are just people, and work to be done, and everybody should do what they can do best. I happen to be a pretty good painter. I'm neat, fast, and sober, and I have a steady hand around windowpanes. Now what my husband is good at is managing." She turned quite serious. "I'm not kidding, Mr. Cromwell. He really is a terribly good manager."

Nice as Mrs. Ferguson was, she was a bit of a nut, too. I guess she would have to be, to live with him. One day when we was working along together and hadn't talked in quite a while, she said, "Mr. Cromwell, there are advantages to anything, if one can find them. There are even advantages to a cracked kitchen wall."

"How do you mean that?" I asked.

"Well," she said, "the worst spot was just above the breakfast table. So I got in the habit of taping up some item of interest there—never said a word about it, just put it there, on top of the crack, and left it awhile, and then put up something else. At the time of the last presidential inauguration, the paper carried a two-page spread of the pictures of all the presidents, and I put that up and left it awhile. Now let me show you the results. Joey!" she called. The seven-year-old showed up, and she said, "Joey, dear, would you like to name the presidents of the United States for Mr. Cromwell?" Joey opened his mouth and said, "George Washington John Adams Thomas Jefferson James Madison James Monroe," and on and on. He stopped for breath once, at Rutherford B. Hayes, but otherwise it just come out in a steady stream. She'd laid down her paintbrush, and she sat there on the top of the ladder, with her little painty paws resting on her spotty gray flannel pants, and a rapt look in her eye. If he'd been mine I'd of kicked him in the pants. Having girls myself who are good-looking like their ma, or will be when they get those damned braces off, little boys give me the creeps anyway. Oh, they look like butter wouldn't melt in their mouths now, but it won't be long.

At this point, the other brat poked his head around a corner and said, "Which president has a name like something to drink?" "You've got me," I said, rather sulky. "Calvin Kool-Aid," said he, and stuck out his tongue and disappeared again. I tell you the Fergusons was a couple of nuts, and they was raising their children to be nuts.

It wasn't just once that Ferguson said I was a artist, but a lot of times, and I guess that was what finally made me decide to show him something I don't show just anybody. One night when I'd come to a good stopping place and was knocking off early, I said, "Mr. Ferguson, you might be interested to know that I do some *real* art work, and maybe you'd like to come over to my house and see it." He looked kind of surprised, but he said he'd be delighted, so we went to my place and I showed him my St. Francises. Lots of people don't realize what you can do with plaster. I make these St. Francises out of plaster, and if I do say so, they're a hell of a lot better than the ones you see in Sears, Roebuck's garden shop. Oh, I pick up some of my ideas from Sears, but if you've ever happened to notice theirs, they don't have any expression in the eyes. Absolutely blank.

I could see Ferguson was stunned. He looked, and he looked, and finally he said, "Mr. Cromwell, when I said you were an artist, I didn't know myself how truly I spoke. Your St. Francises are in a class by themselves."

He seemed to like them so much that I told him I'd give him one for his front yard. He said, "Mr. Cromwell, I deeply appreciate that kind thought. But, between ourselves, Mrs. Ferguson, while a fine woman, is a black Protestant, and I just don't know how she'd take to a St. Francis peering out so expressively from amid the petunias. This is something that will take preliminary spadework, Mr. Cromwell." I guess he never talked her into it, because I never heard anything further, which goes to show how narrow-minded even nice people can be. It's a question of early training.

And speaking of early training, my artistic interests go right back to grade school. I was in Room 206, which was where they put the dummies to get us out of the smart kids' way. We done lots of basket weaving in 206. Considerable rug hooking. Knitting. Crocheting. It give me a lifelong interest in the useful arts. Not all the kids in 206 turned out to be as dumb as you might think, either. One of my best friends in 206 is working on his second quarter-million in the used-car business, and there is absolutely nothing wrong with his arithmetic. One of the smart kids who was in school the same time as us works for him, putting a new tread on tires that have wore smooth, which is a real tough way to make a buck.

I finally got toward the end of Ferguson's job, and one evening I mentioned to him that I'd be looking for some more evening jobs, in case he happened to hear of any. He said he'd keep it in mind. "However, Mr. Cromwell," he said, "I don't like to think of you going on like this working days and evenings both. This is no life for a man of your breadth of interests." I said well, for right now I needed to, and there it was. He didn't say anything for a while, and then he cocked his head to one side and asked, "Have you ever done any plastering in Georgetown, Mr. Cromwell?" I said no, I hadn't ever happened to. He looked thoughtful and said, "Georgetown, Mr. Cromwell, must be a gold mine of plaster cracks."

Well, you know about Georgetown. At least everybody around Washington, D.C., does. It's the old section of Washington, full of people like Kennedys and Secretaries of State, and a big newspaper columnist or two, and a few artists and writers, but only those who inherited money and wash regular, along with some who regard the lot of them as newcomers. Some of the smaller places are peed a tares for people who mainly live on fox-hunting estates out in Virginia. I never heard that George Washington himself slept in any of those Georgetown houses, but he sure knew people who did. Row houses is what they are, most of them—they rise up straight and narrow, with their front doors resting their lower lips right on the sidewalk, and each one has in the back a little walled yard, about the size of a pocket handkerchief, with three bushes surrounded by imported pebbles. When one of those Georgetown houses needs fixing, they don't repair it, they restore it, with bricks two hundred years old and worm-eaten timbers, if they can get ahold of any.

What's funny about Georgetown—at least it's funny if you don't live there yourself—is that out-of-towners look at it and think it's a nice clean slum. There's a story about some prominent lady from New York who was driven through Georgetown and looked out at those little old row houses, none of which you couldn't touch for I reckon much under seventy or a hundred thousand, and said, "My, isn't it sweet to see the poor keep up their homes so nicely!" Well, I don't know whether that's true. They tell it all the time. But I do know something else is true, because it was in all the papers a couple of years back. There was a bunch of visiting teachers from Italy—they was English teachers—who was coming here for a summer to improve their English under some kind of grant or something, and some of the Georgetown ladies, who are great for hands across the sea and all like that, each invited a teacher to stay with them for the summer. The Italian teachers looked at the houses they was being invited to live in and balked. They said they didn't want to stay in slums like that, they wanted to stay in some nice, modern place. They said they didn't think they would hear a good class of English spoke in a section of town like that.

Well, anyway, I had to agree with Ferguson that there was probably plenty of plaster cracks in Georgetown. He was quiet for a good while, and seemed to be doing some hard thinking, and after a bit I see him with pencil and paper. Pretty soon he said, "Mr. Cromwell, I think I have it. We are going to catch the Georgetown trade! This ad will go in the *Washington Post,* but *not* in the classified section, Mr. Cromwell! This will go in the editorial section, over to the right of Joseph Alsop, I think." He beamed and rubbed his hands together, happy as a ten-year-old with a new yo-yo, and then he handed it to me with a flourish. He had set it up in a frilly little box, all neatly printed and spaced, and it said:

COLONIAL CRAFTSMEN

Restorations of Historic Plaster

Our work is done exclusively by
hand by highly skilled artisans.
A preliminary analysis of your
plaster and recommendations
concerning its restoration will be
made at a nominal fee. Calls for
appointments are accepted only
from 6:30 P.M. to 8:30 P.M.
JA 9-4623

I looked at that ad, and I didn't say anything for a few minutes. I was just holding myself together. Finally I said, very calm and careful, "Mr. Ferguson, I am sure you know your own line of work, whatever that may be. I don't believe you've ever happened to mention. But believe me, you don't know plastering, and that ain't the way to get no plastering jobs. Why, that ad don't say anything about sober, or experienced, or work guaranteed, and as for all this business about analysis and recommendations at a nominal fee, by which I reckon you mean estimate, well, Mr. Ferguson, you can't charge people *anything* for making a estimate! And exclusively by hand! Mr. Ferguson, *all* plastering's handwork! They ain't invented a machine yet that can plaster! And that ain't my phone number you put down there, that's yours. And besides everything else, Mr. Ferguson, I don't know what a ad like that would cost, but plenty, I bet, and I can't afford it."

Ferguson said, "Mr. Cromwell, you leave this thing to me, if you don't mind. To take up only some of your objections, I do not recommend your using the word *sober*. One hopes that the surgeon who removes one's appendix will be sober, but it's not a point one raises. As to guaranteeing your work, I do not advise it. Not in Georgetown. Those old houses shift from one foot to another all day long as the traffic rattles by on those cobblestone streets. No, I definitely do not advise guaranteeing anything. As to the cost of this ad, you're not paying for it; I am. And if that makes you feel badly, Mr. Cromwell, there are a few cracks, which I don't believe I've mentioned, in the upstairs back bedroom. Perhaps you wouldn't mind, purely as a favor, just slapping a little plaster in them, as it were."

Slapping a little plaster in a few cracks! If it wasn't that Ferguson could outtalk me, so that I was beat before I started, I would of balked when I seen that upstairs back bedroom. The plaster looked like a detail map of the Mississippi and tributaries. And they was the kind of cracks that when you start to clean them out so you can get some plaster in them, they spread right on across the wall. I worked on that bedroom a week, getting sorer and sorer at what I'd got myself into that I wasn't getting a red cent for. Oh, I cut a few corners, as many as I could with that buzzard Ferguson peering over my shoulder, but even so it was a awful job.

It was about the middle of the week when that ad of Ferguson's got in the paper, and that evening Ferguson had just come in the door and laid down his *Wall Street Journal* when the telephone rang. He took it on the upstairs extension, and I heard him saying "Yas?" There was a long pause, with Ferguson saying "Mm" in a medical kind of way from time to time. Then he said, his English accent so thick it was practically strangling him, "Ah, yas, Mrs. Abbott, for a situation such as you describe, I *wish* I could give you our Mr. Cromwell, a magnificent artisan, in fact, I may say an artist. He has an understanding of plahstah of the type you have described such as few attain. But unfohtunately Mr. Cromwell is all tied up at the moment with the restoration of an old Virginia mahnsion. A piddy. Ah, but just a moment, just a moment! Perhaps something *could* be worked out! Mmm. Mrs. Abbott, I believe our Mr. Cromwell could come to you a week from Choosday. At six in the evening. Not at all, Mrs. Abbott, not at all. Only too heppy."

Ferguson took three or four more calls that same evening, and it went on that way the rest of the week. By the time I finished Ferguson's bedroom he had ten or twelve estimating appointments lined up for me.

Well, the rest, as they say, is history. Two weeks later I shook the plaster dust of Brown Bros. Construction off my shoes and was in business for myself. Now I've got twelve men working under me and a English girl to answer the phone, and things are going right well. I've even sold two St. Francises for them Georgetown back gardens. They're *primitives,* which made me kind of mad at first, but I found out it don't mean anything. It's just a word.

I'd been thinking about Ferguson, and then one day he called me up. He asked me how things were going, and I told him fine. "I trust that Mrs. Cromwell is in good spirits?" he asked. "She hasn't a complaint in the world," I said, which was true; Genevieve has even got to where she don't mind if I have a drink now and then, seeing the class of clientele I associate with. I asked how Mrs. Ferguson was, and he said, "In fine fettle, Mr. Cromwell, in fine fettle. She is now repapering the hall. I know good work when I see it, Mr. Cromwell, and I can say without fear of exaggeration that when it comes to paperhanging Mrs. Ferguson is without peer. The eye that woman has for matching a pattern!" Then he got down to business. "Mr.

Cromwell, the kitchen wall is doing splendidly. It was your masterwork. In fact, the whole downstairs is most satisfactory. But I regret that I cannot say as much for the upstairs back bedroom. It simply is not holding up. Cracks are reappearing rapidly, Mr. Cromwell."

"Mr. Ferguson," I said, "as you may know, Colonial Craftsmen does not guarantee their work, owing to the unpredictable effects of atmospheric conditions upon delicate handwork of this type. However, I believe that at the time we restored your home we *were* offering guarantees, and Colonial's word is as good as its bond. I shall send you our Mr. Saskiewicz, a old-world artisan."

Saskiewicz worked on that upstairs back bedroom the better part of a week, and when he come back his nerves was all shot to pieces. But he must of done a good job. I never heard another squawk out of Ferguson.

His Beautiful Handwriting

It was when I couldn't sleep, the other night, that I started wondering, my mind scurrying along the narrow dark streets of the past, *why didn't I ever tell Bill that his handwriting was beautiful?* His dark head bent above his work, his flat, expressionless eyes raised halfway, not all the way to meet mine, he paused in making the big, beautiful rounded letters as I came by his desk. We hardly spoke to each other. Why didn't I ever say anything about this one thing, this only thing he could do well? I guess I was too ignorant, too uncertain, half afraid of him, too preoccupied with thirty other children. Nobody ever told me what I should say to Bill. Certainly not Miss Mary Frances Chips, as I shall call her.

I am sitting, with another girl, named, I think, Flora Christian, in a little edge-of-the-campus coffee shop. She is not a special friend of mine, but we have just emerged from Miss Mary Frances Chips's class in elementary education. I don't know whether we often go over for a Coke together, or whether this is an isolated occasion. She is a redheaded, sloe-eyed drama student. We walk in the shop and sit down, and across the shop, facing me on the newsstand, is a monster headline: KING ABDICATES FOR "WOMAN I LOVE."

"The king has abdicated!" I cry to Flora.

"What king?" asks Flora.

Her mind had been tempered in the refining fire of Miss Mary Frances Chips's class, and it is sharp as a steel blade. We are very fortunate to be in Miss Mary Frances Chips's section of elementary education, and we know it. Miss Chips is a Lovely Person, and the elementary schools of half the state are staffed by products of her course. The first thing we do in her class is to learn an alphabetical list of words, headed by the statement "A teacher is . . ."

Miss Chips presents this list disarmingly, the hamminess of it presented like a sandwich, with a layer of smiling sophistication winking at us on top of it, and on top of that a layer of sobriety. I know that this may seem like a rather absurd service by which to learn to be a teacher, Miss Chips seems to say to us, but I am serious; I want you to memorize it; there are some absurd devices that work. And so we learn them, and Miss Chips lectures on them for some weeks.

But not exclusively. Not exclusively. Miss Mary Frances Chips digresses from time to time. She had gone to the University of Chicago at one time, and the class had been seated alphabetically. She discovered that she was seated next to Mr. Chester, and (here Miss Chips lowered her voice confidentially) "Mr. Chester, class, was a Big, Black, Negro Man!" Miss Chips, always the lady, made no public fuss, but after the class she went up to the teacher and she explained to him that she couldn't sit there. The teacher said, "Miss Chips, you southern girls will just have to adjust yourselves to our ways, I am afraid. The seating arrangement cannot be changed." Miss Chips smiled gently at us, and she sighed and said, "And so I sat theah for a whole semester, since I wanted that course. Ah didn't like it, and ah wouldn't have done it for any other course, but for that one I did." And she smiled, and sighed again, and she picked up her glasses and put them on and went back to lecturing on A Teacher Is Industrious.

She never says anything about what to do with Bill, and I don't ask, for I don't know, yet, of his existence.

He is a little boy now, slower than the rest; people are already puzzled about him; they have discovered that Bill is not very bright. He treads the pathway of his life, plodding slowly along, toward me, and my path—back and forth to Miss Mary Frances Chips's education class, and across the street to the Coke shop, and to the dormitory for dinner—is leading me slowly to him.

And the day comes, finally, when I stand, young and scared and uncertain about the whole thing, in front of a class of thirty eight-year-olds, and there is Bill. I am alert, but I am also afraid, as I see those flat dark eyes that never look all the way to my face; the head that is always at a slightly hangdog angle, the sort of sulky, stupid sweetness of his face, that intense quietness. Bill is no trouble; he never talks in class, he never makes any difficulty; he sits there, unable to read, unable to do anything, except to write, to copy big, beautiful *e*'s and *l*'s and *j*'s. He has been handed along by teachers thus far; they, too, don't know what to do with him. I am Mrs. Squeers, and he is Spike. I am cruel to him in my very ignoring him, my leaving him alone. And why, why in God's name, did I never tell him he wrote beautifully? Would that quiet, sober face have broken into one smile? Had anyone ever tried it? What do you think, Miss Mary Frances Chips?

Yankee Traders

Sometimes they would get in the car and drive around the country for a weekend, or a week, or even longer. Julia's objective on these excursions, if they were in a part of the country that had antique shops, was old-fashioned pearl-handled fruit knives. It so happens that pearl-handled fruit knives, while not really qualifying as a rarity, are very hard to come by. Sometimes they got within smelling distance of them; sometimes they would inquire at some respectable old New England farmhouse with a genteel sign under the maple tree in the front yard saying "Antiques," and the lady would exclaim, What a shame! She had just last week sold a simply beautiful set, in perfect condition. Or sometimes an old gentleman proprietor of an odds-and-ends shop would cackle, Why, sure! He had a very fine set, and Julia's nostrils would quiver with the delight of a hunter closing in on the prey; but when he shuffled out with them from the back room, they would be pearl-handled butter knives. "Oh, *fruit* knives," he would say with surprise and a faint air of disparagement. "You ain't goin' to find any of them so easy; I sold the ones that went with these about a year ago to a dealer over to Waterford." Sometimes they would drive miles out of their way on little country roads because they had been told that three miles past the Eastburyport Unitarian Church, turn to your right, and one mile past the Westburyport Unified Presbyterians, down the hill, jog to the north and at the foot of the rainbow, lived Mrs. Silas Perkins, who had a set of fruit knives she had said last spring she didn't get any use out of. But they were never there; always Mrs. Silas Perkins had already disposed of them.

John would himself get so caught up in the spirit of the chase, so intent on prising out of people all they knew about where fruit knives might be found, so interested in testing the accuracy of the directions that he was given, that he would quite forget to object to the whole project. But once in a while the absurdity of it all would come over him, and he would say to Julia, "Why do you want pearl-handled fruit knives, anyway?" "Oh," she would say vaguely, "they're nice if you want to serve somebody fruit—after all, it's awkward to pass the kitchen paring knife around." "Personally, I eat the skins," John would say fretfully. Anyway, he would add, although he had never actually seen a pearl-handled fruit knife, he gathered that they were simply little silver knives, and so he didn't see any reason why they should be particularly good for paring anything anyway. She would say, even more vaguely, that that didn't really matter. The truth was that she didn't much care whether she ever acquired any pearl-handled fruit knives or not; it was simply a good reason for stopping when you were tired of driving, and for poking into people's houses and for getting into conversations with people. They provided some objective, some purpose, to a ramble around the country; and since they were never to be found, they could last indefinitely as an objective.

"But what on earth will you do if you find some?" John asked once.

"I suppose I shall have to buy them, and then we'll have to find something else to look for," she said.

And as they looked for pearl-handled fruit knives, the trunk and the backseat of the car filled up with things that all the people who didn't have pearl-handled fruit knives *did* have.

"It's a shame neither of us likes fish much," John said as he carefully stowed a Sheffield fish set (both beautiful and a tremendous bargain) in the backseat next to a footstool on which was printed in lurching nail holes, "Presented to John Garfield Harrison, 80 years old, May 5, 1890, by the Volunteer Fire Department." "In fact," John said, "hunting for fruit knives is an expensive hobby."

"But at least it's a sport that doesn't take any special equipment," Julia said. "Look at the people who hunt deer or fish or something—all those rifles and dry flies or whatever. And then look at all the people we meet—all these New Englanders."

For example, take the lady in New Beaumont, Massachusetts. She was an aristocrat among antique dealers, stylishly stout, snugly encased in gold knitted wool, her white hair becomingly blued, her lipstick handsomely vivid. She didn't have any fruit knives. Julia picked up a dish and inspected it, and John scrutinized a chest of drawers, muttering in a professional way (one learns the trick of these things) "Quite a nice piece, but not really old, of course—paneled ends."

"But beautiful," said the lady authoritatively. "In fact, we had that piece in our own home, when we were in the larger place, of course, and naturally we had only the best, not all the same period, of course, since some of the things were inherited from the Bradfords, and others had been added later by the Russells. Perhaps you know of Henry Russell," she added. "He wrote the first law textbook used by Hahvahd College. Or perhaps you wouldn't know, what *is* your field, if I may ask?"

"Economics," said John, moving to a Chinese whatnot.

"Oh, *economics*!" she cried. "Why just the other day a young economics professor from Hahvahd was here looking at that very piece. . . . I really don't know why it is, but the younger intellectuals seem to like the Chinese sort of thing very much. Of course, as a matter of fact, I do myself. In fact, perhaps you don't know it, but there is quite a New England tradition of Chinese along with the Early American—the early sea captains, don't you know. . . . But where *are* you from?"

"Just outside of Washington," said Julia.

"*Washington!*" cried the lady. "My dear, we are practically Washington residents ourselves. Where do you live?"

"Virginia," said Julia.

"Oh, one of those fine old homes in Alexandria, of course," said the lady generously. "Why, my dear, we have a home in Alexandria ourselves—I go there in winters. My husband, of course, is there all the time, the Capitol, of course—"

"No," said John firmly, interrupting. "We live in Arlington."

"Arlington?" said the lady. "Well," she said graciously, "I'm sure there are some fine old homes in Arlington *too* . . . of course you know of my husband, he used to be the director of Atomic Energy. . . ."

"Oh, you're Mrs. Lilienthal?" John said politely.

"Certainly not," she said stiffly. "Johnson, well, as I was saying, of course we have one of the really old places in Alexandria . . . I don't know whether you've had the opportunity . . ."

"Then you must know the Harleys," said Julia, reaching around in her mind for a weapon. "They have what is considered, I believe, to be the finest of the old Alexandria homes. I think they were persuaded to open it last year for one of those charity purposes or something of the sort. . . ."

"*Tours,* my dear," said the lady, "why, they have simply begged me and *begged* me to place our home on tour, quite worthy causes of course, but I simply will *not*—why our carpets *alone,* with the public tracking mud in and all that sort of thing. No, my dear," she said, shaking her head reprovingly at Julia, "I simply cannot place our home on tour!"

"What," said John, "is that sort of . . . uh . . . hanging up there?" He pointed at a cloth affair, perhaps six feet long and two and a half feet wide, hung from the rafters. Appliquéd with neat little embroidery stitches on a tannish background were three brilliantly colored Egyptianlike figures, in profile, facing west, one of whom seemed to be carrying a sacrificial lamb; and one Egyptianlike figure, in profile, faced east and seemed to be carrying a shepherd's crook. At the top was a line of mysterious-looking picture writing, neatly appliquéd in letters about six inches high.

"Oh *no!*" exclaimed the lady. "Do you know, I was afraid, simply from the moment you came in, that your eye might fall on that. We had it in our own home, of course, when we were in the larger place, and in fact when I put it here in the shop, I told my husband *purposely* to hang it from the rafters, veddy, *veddy* high so that no one would notice it. I cannot *bear,* I told my husband—those were my very words—I cannot *bear* for anyone to take that away from me."

"What is it exactly?" asked John, looking interested.

"Phoenican," said the lady promptly. "Or Assyrian. I can *never* remember. But there was a young Hahvahd professor who told me that he was quite sure it was one or the other, I forget which, and he was, of course, *quite* sure that it was priceless. It is strange how the young intellectual type immediately sees that hanging—other people simply never notice— and the moment I saw you, I knew somehow that you might notice—in fact, if I may say so, I *feared* that you might notice it. The young Hahvahd professor told me that I really *should* take it to the Metropolitan Museum and have it studied, positively identified, you know, or possibly to the Smithsonian. But I have never done it, very careless of me, but I simply liked it for itself. When I had it in our own home, I frequently said to guests who admired it that I was sure it was really a very valuable museum piece, but it wasn't for that reason I had it—I had it because it *spoke* to me. That's the way we New Englanders are—the things the sea captains brought in at all, priceless museum pieces, and yet we simply have them because . . . You know," she interrupted herself, turning the full force of her dazzling smile on John, "the moment your eye fell on it, I could see that it spoke to *you*!"

"I think," said Julia, "that some enterprising New England schoolgirl sat down thirty or forty years ago and appliquéd a copy of a picture she saw in her ancient history book."

"A *copy*!" cried the lady. "My dear," she said stiffly, "I *have* no copies in this shop; I have nothing but originals. Why even my Chinese rose plates—many people cannot *believe* that they are original—why, not even the Metropolitan Museum has a *full* set of originals. No, my dear"—turning her back on Julia—"I can assure you that it is *not* a copy."

"I meant," said Julia placatingly, "a copy of something made in 2000 B.C. or something like that, after all you could hardly expect . . ."

"As a matter of fact," said John to Julia, laughing, "it does rather speak to me."

"Maybe you and it had better go off and have a nice long conversation together," said Julia sourly.

"My dear," said the lady, turning coldly to Julia, "I *do not* allow my things to be taken by people who don't really care for them. As a matter of fact, the very same young Hahvahd professor I was mentioning to you wanted that piece, but his wife didn't care for it. It simply didn't *speak* to her. He really felt quite badly about it, in fact, he drops in now and then just to look at it again, but I have told him, 'No, you must not take it; I cannot *allow* you to take it. You must look for something—no doubt you will find *something*—that speaks to your wife also. This is a piece which must be cherished; I had it in my own home for years, and I assure you, I simply *cherished* it.' "

"Well," said Julia defensively. "I quite *like* it. I mean, I think it's quite handsome. But I just don't know what a person would *do* with it."

"How much is it?" asked John.

"Ten dollars," said the lady briefly.

"What do you think?" said John to Julia.

"Oh, take it," said Julia.

"Oh, I don't know," said John nervously. "After all, it's pretty hard to get it down from there. I don't know as it's really worth the bother. . . ."

"Absolutely no bother at all," said the lady briskly. With startling agility, she whisked out a stepladder, sprang up it, and in no time was high above them, untacking it with a hammer. Words floated down: "Of course, I shall miss it, in fact, my *husband* shall miss it, but I do feel happy when I know that my things will be cherished. . . ." She rolled it up, unobtrusively brushing off a few cobwebs and shaking out a bit of dust, and they stowed it in the backseat next to the fish set.

As they drove off, she stood there drying the ten-dollar check in the breeze and waving graciously at them. "I know that you will enjoy it," she shouted. "Why, when it was hanging in my own home . . ." The rest was lost.

They drove along the road in silence. Finally John said, "Well, it *did* speak to me!"

And then there was the lady who made hooked rugs. They had stopped at a house that had a sign saying "Antiques" out in front. The lady of the house was past middle age, a tired woman in a faded cotton dress who was pathetically eager to sell the few bits of milk glass and china plates and bric-a-brac that were sitting around her respectable, faded living room, as her stock-in-trade, but she was too unaccustomed to urging anything of hers on others, too polite, to be a good saleswoman. No, she didn't have any fruit knives. As they were leaving, Julia commented on the pretty hooked rug on her floor, really mostly to have something pleasant to say; she somehow felt that this was what tourists did all day long—they stopped and looked indifferently at her few little wares and went quickly on their way, until the woman, who had perhaps put the sign up at the beginning of the season in a burst of hopeful enterprise, no longer expected anything else, but still tiredly left her kitchen or her mending to answer the doorbell.

"It is pretty, ain't it," the woman answered. "Somebody made it for my mother years ago. You can't get very many nice hooked rugs anymore, the way the old folks made them—people haven't got the time anymore, I guess. I only know one woman, way out in the country east of here, that still makes them. Beautiful things, they are. In fact, one of them was taken down to the state legislature last session and exhibited."

Their interest in hooked rugs had been minimal; but as she talked, their mouths watered, their nostrils quivered. With a single voice, they said casually, "I wonder if she ever makes them for other people."

"Yes," she said, "I think she does sometimes."

"Where does she live?" they asked. The woman told them; it seemed that you took the little unimproved road over to Millvale, and then it was best to ask there how to get to Mrs. Bert Thomas's; it was a complicated route, and she couldn't tell them exactly, but the one thing she *did* know was that it was the steepest road out to the Thomases' farm she had ever been on. "Land!" she said. "I was over there last winter, and I never thought we'd make it over that road. But it won't be so bad now, when it's summer and all."

They bounced over the rocky Vermont road, and

laughed at the idea of going all this way to look at hooked rugs, even possibly one that had been exhibited at the Vermont State Legislature. But it was sort of fun; how else would they ever have found themselves in the backwoods of Vermont, on their way to a Vermont farmhouse to see a genuine, aboriginal maker of hooked rugs, untutored by home demonstration agents, unsullied by traffic with rug dealers? "Anyway," Julia said, "we don't have to buy a hooked rug, even if she's willing to sell one. I don't see that it's really taking advantage just to go and look because we heard they were so beautiful." "Of course not," said John.

At Millvale they inquired, and found that Mrs. Bert Thomas had to be distinguished from the Seth Thomases, the *young* Mrs. Bert Thomas, the *old*, old Mrs. Bert Thomas, and the Jim Thomases. By slow degrees they narrowed the circle and closed in on the proper and genuine Mrs. Bert Thomas. Up a winding road they went, according to their instructions, through the pretty Vermont countryside, past a deserted quarry, past a pond, past a "four corners," and finally the little road narrowed, and over the last steep little hill it ended at an old white stone farmhouse. They pulled up beside a low stone porch, and there on the porch was a pretty sight; a ruddy, healthy old woman, with her clean, almost white hair twisted up in a knot at the top of her head, her sleeves rolled up to show strong brown arms, working on a hooked rug, with balls of yarn strewn here and there on the stone floor. A calico cat, too old to be interested in playing with the yarn, paused in washing his ears and looked up at them.

"We came because we heard you made beautiful hooked rugs," said Julia.

"Well," said Mrs. Bert Thomas, "I may look like I was makin' one right now, but I ain't. This is an old rug, supposed to be real valuable, that an antique dealer over to Burlington asked me if I would repair. Frankly," she said, lowering her voice, "it's in such turrible shape it ain't worth all the trouble to match them faded old colors and all. I don't know whether it's going to hold after I get it mended; it's just plain rotten. I could practically make a new one in the time this takes. And I ain't really got much time anyhow, because I've got to do so much outside work since Pa's been so sick and can't do much around the farm. Now you take today—I been raking after the mower all morning, and I just now got back to this rug job."

She was perfect; she was lovely. Their tongues hung out; they panted to buy a hooked rug from her.

"Do you have any rugs of your own you're interested in selling?" Julia asked.

"Not a one," said Mrs. Bert Thomas cheerfully. "I been cleaned out lately. But why don't you come in anyhow, seeing as you've come so far and up that hill and all. I'll show you a couple of rugs I've got here that are sold but the folks haven't come for them yet."

Sadly, but still feeling rather flattered, they followed her inside, and she showed them the rugs—big, gay, and unquestionably handsome affairs. In the background hovered Pa, a thin, stooped old shadow of a man who looked all the frailer beside her.

"Now you just sit down and visit a while," said Mrs. Thomas hospitably. "By the way," she said casually, "maybe you're interested in aprons—my daughter Bella makes aprons." From somewhere she whisked out a collection of gay aprons. "She only takes a dollar apiece for them," Mrs. Thomas said casually. "Just sort of something to pick up at odd moments, she just loves to sew. Now, this one, I think, is real pretty. I told Bella, 'Bella,' I said, 'you oughtn't to sell this one, it's just too pretty to part with.' "

"As a matter of fact," Julia said to John, "I always am short of aprons."

"Well, you certainly ought to get some," said John absently, his eye wandering over the clean house, like the interior in a Dutch painting.

"Well, I'll take this one," said Julia, snatching at the one Mrs. Thomas didn't think Bella ought to sell, "and this one, and John, don't you think this one is pretty?"

"Sure, sure," said John, "take them all."

"Maybe you'd like the one Bella is just working on," said Mrs. Thomas. "It's real pretty, I don't know but what it's prettier than these. Oh, Bella!" she roared. "Have you finished that yellow apron?"

"Just about, Ma," called back Bella, and in a minute she came in the room, biting off the thread on a yellow apron as she came. She was a hefty young woman who looked like a slightly coarser version of her mother.

"Now, I noticed you looking this house over," Mrs. Thomas said to John. "I guess you can see it's real old. It's about a hundred and fifty years old. I bet," she said generously, "you'd be interested to take a look at our cellar, lots of people think it's real interesting."

"Why, yes," they said, flattered.

Mrs. Thomas led the way down a crooked little stone stairway to the cellar, a dark, very cold stone place. "Mind the stairs," she said. "You can see this has been here a real long time. It's a wonderful place for storing food—I keep butter down here just as good as anybody could in a refrigerator. I do a lot of canning," she said casually, waving a hand at neat, provident rows of beautiful orange carrots and purple beets in glass quart jars. "All those come right out of my garden, tender little baby things with the dew still on 'em. I canned an awful lot, more'n we can use, but I just couldn't let them go to waste. Sometimes when people want them I let them go for thirty-five cents a jar," she added.

Julia's good fortune almost overwhelmed her. The idea that she could take home some of these beautiful jars, from this beautiful cold stone cellar, a hundred and fifty years old, put up by Mrs. Bert Thomas, seemed too good to be true. "Oh, John," she said, "we should take some."

At that moment Mrs. Thomas's son Josh came down to the cellar. He was a local auctioneer who had just returned from conducting an auction, still with his tall hat on and his auctioneer's frock, which hung loosely on his tall thin frame.

Mrs. Thomas performed the introductions. Josh was a very jovial but sharp-eyed young man who fixed his eye on John and his armful of jars and eagerly offered to carry them to the car, suggesting a few more. John replied lamely that he would love to take all he could but that there was no room in the trunk for any more. Whereupon Josh asked for the keys, assuring John that he would take care of everything. Soon he returned with the keys and cheerfully announced that he had found plenty of room for additional jars.

As they climbed out of the cellar, they were almost blinded by the brilliant early afternoon sunshine, which basked the farm in a warm radiant glow. They were about to say good-bye when Josh asked genially, "You wouldn't be interested in buying the farm, would you?"

"Why, is it for sale?" asked John.

"Well, yes, I guess it is," Mrs. Thomas said reluctantly.

"Land, we'd a stayed here forever if it wasn't for Pa's health. But it's just getting too much for us. Like I told you, this house is a hundred and fifty years old, and just as solid as the day it was built, and we've got a sawmill right here on the place"—she waved at a rather dilapidated building of some sort on her right— "and a fine stand of timber—why, land, the money to be made off of timber these days!"

"What do you raise here?" asked Julia.

"Anything!" cried Mrs. Thomas. "Absolutely anything! The most fertile soil you'll ever see." She waved expansively at a field to the right of her, where, through a sparse sprinkling of dirt, the solid Vermont rock showed through. Enchanted, they followed her gaze. "And the view!" Mrs. Thomas said. "Why, every morning I get up and look across them hills, and I thank the Good Lord that I can see a sight like that." She smiled at them a little shyly, embarrassed a trifle by her own poetry. They, too, looked across the blue hills, and poetry welled up in their souls.

"How much are you asking for the farm?" asked John, trying to get hold of himself.

"Twelve thousand dollars," said Mrs. Thomas. "It's forty acres."

It was incredible. That fertile soil, those God-given hills, the hundred-and-fifty-year-old house, all for a mere twelve thousand dollars. They looked at each other in a panic, wondering wildly whether Mrs. Thomas would mind the fact that they didn't happen to have twelve thousand dollars on them at the moment, and whether she would be willing to hold it for them until they could get to the bank.

But finally John seized Julia by the arm and said, "We must go." "We will think about the farm," he called loudly to the Thomases as he was getting into the car. "In the meantime let me pay for the jars." Whereupon Josh whisked out a pad and pencil from his pocket and started to list all the jars he so solicitously placed in the trunk. The total came to $12.60, nearly ten times more than John originally contemplated. Taken aback by the figure, John was about to protest when he realized that originally he almost invited Josh to put all the jars he could find room for in the trunk and could not now ask him to take them out. He therefore meekly paid the sum Josh had calculated, and taking Julia by the arm almost pushed her into the car.

They didn't talk as they bounced down the steep, winding road. Finally, when they had got back on the main route, John said, "You know, about those glass jars of carrots and beets that she said were little baby ones. As a matter of fact, those are great big old tough carrots and beets—I had a good look at them when I took them off the shelves."

They drove on in silence awhile. Finally Julia said shortly, "Well, they spoke to me."

I

The old woman, who was ninety-two, lay high on the hospital bed that had been installed in her room, and with dim, wandering eyes looked out across the fields beyond her window. The fields started at the picket fence of the yard and stretched out, plain and flat, to the horizon, where they suddenly disappeared in a mirage, a shimmering strip of blue in which some faraway farmer's barn and windmill floated. The mirage was the only decoration, the only useless thing in the landscape; it gave people the idea, which they never put into words, that they lived within sight of the sea, although the Gulf of Mexico was, in reality, out of sight, around the curve of the earth.

Looking out of the window, the old woman worried about the drought; if it didn't rain, she thought, the fields would dry up, and the cattle would starve, and what would become of them all? She sometimes worried out loud to the practical nurse, who sat in a rocking chair at the foot of the bed and read *The Woman's Home Companion*. The nurse, Mrs. Ewing, would say cheerfully, "There isn't any drought, Grandma. We've had real nice rains this fall." This was not entirely true, just as many of the things Mrs. Ewing said so cheerfully were not.

The old woman would turn her eyes disconsolately back to the window, uncomforted, for she knew that something was wrong, that something was impending; when something had been wrong, it had usually been the drought, and if it was not the drought now, what could it be?

She had come from across the ocean to this dry land before she could remember, and she had learned to fear the drought when she was very young; and so the worry often led her backward in time. Sometimes it would drift away, and she would be sixteen again, lighthearted and light-footed, waltzing in wild, dizzy whirls. Bright, laughing young faces looked down at her as they waltzed, and she smiled up at them; one of them belonged to Emil Hartwig, whose ring, a wide, dull gold band, covered one of her shrunken old fingers almost to the knuckle. He had been dead for over sixty years. And sometimes, a plump young widow, she would be waltzing again, a shade more decorously, and the face that looked down at her would be John Heldt's. His wide gold band shone on another finger; he had been dead for almost fifty years. Waltzing, waltzing, her feet moved a little under the covers; Mrs. Ewing noticed it, and got up and put an afghan across them. "No circulation," she thought. "Her poor old feet are probably getting chilly."

But she wasn't waltzing anymore now. She was worrying about her daughter Anna, her plain, timid Anna, who had never learned how to smile up at a man and to make the most of herself. She was hoping Anna wasn't going to throw herself away on Jim Holmes.

II

In the kitchen, Anna finished the last of the breakfast dishes and leaned her thin, tired, girlish body against the sink, looking out of the big kitchen window, as she had done for forty years. Had anyone said to her that the view of the flat converging fields, stretching away to the horizon without a hiding place, was a dull and uninteresting landscape, she would have exclaimed in shy surprise. From that window she saw at dusk her old yellow tomcat disappear into the western fields, caterwauling as he went, to return meekly the following morning, with some of the fur missing from one ear, and vowing reform; the old mother hen hunting for worms in the pasture with her flock of adolescent turkeys, puzzling over the enormous children she had raised; the foolish black-and-white dog snubbed by the cat and returning to be snubbed again; and the mockingbird couple, who nested each year in the fig tree that branched across the window, struggling to keep up with the voracious appetites of their young. The flowerbed by the picket fence was hers; she had planted it. The fig tree that spread across the window was hers; Jim had planted it for her twenty years ago, and the great live oak beyond had grown from the sapling they had planted together, forty years ago. The landscape was theirs, hers and Jim's, and forty years ago it had been only a low, wild tangle of mesquite brush, which no man's foot had ever touched, for never had so much as an Indian arrowhead been turned up in all those acres. Sometimes she felt a great sense of accomplishment, for they had done what people had been doing from the beginning of time, turning a piece of wilderness into a home. But at other times she thought, "Well, it's all we've done with our lives, too— that and raise three children." For she was old; she was seventy-three.

It was time she stopped mooning and thought about lunch. Lunch for Jim didn't matter too much. Once she had said to her daughter, Margaret, laughing, "I had plenty of advice about what kind of man to marry, so I won't give you but one piece: Don't marry a man who's fussy about his food. Your father may have his faults, but he'll make his lunch of leftovers and not say a word, if I feel like working in the garden instead of cooking."

But now there was Mrs. Ewing, a woman with the look of one who expects a substantial lunch. And, anyway, Margaret was home. Margaret wasn't fussy, but since she now lived so far away and was home so seldom, her mother felt that she should be treated a little like company. Anna took a last look out the window, scanning the sky for rain clouds, and then took out the flour and shortening and began to make a piecrust.

III

In the living room, Margaret dusted the furniture with quick, tense, furious gestures. This place, she thought irritably, is dusty, littered, cluttered with memories—and most of them didn't even matter. They had been laid away in mothballs, they were useless and irrelevant, not even worth taking out and sorting over; she would like to donate them in a lump to some Salvation Army of things past, with the virtuous thought that

someone poverty-stricken in memory—a worthy am-
nesiac, perhaps—might get some good out of them.

In the front yard that she could see through the
windows, she had, when she was nine or ten, worried
about stepping on ants. She couldn't help stepping on
an ant occasionally; the world was full of ants. But
how did the ants feel about it, she had wondered.
Would they wait up long for him in the anthill to-
night? Down the road that she could see in the distance, she had once walked to school. In the early
spring, which came briefly at the end of February, before the long, dry, hot summer set in, the edges of the
road and the pastures beyond had been gloriously covered with wildflowers, coarse, garish, hopeful yellow
things that had no names, and had never had poetry
written about them, and showed the effects. She had
almost danced down that road to school with delight
in the color that surrounded her; and, arriving there,
had read of the fringed gentian and the early crocus,
the field of yellow daffodils and the daisy turned up by
the plow. She had never seen any of these, but she believed in them dutifully; and once in the fifth grade she
and the other children had been required to sweat out
a few verses about the daffodil themselves.

But none of it mattered; she was weary of remembering it. She had come home because her grandmother was dying. She had said, back in the city

suburb with Roger and their friends, "Well, I guess I simply have to go down and try to cheer up the old things a little." She could not say that she was going home because her grandmother was dying, for it would have sounded almost humorous, like the proverbial excuse of the office boy who wants to see the baseball game.

But almost the earliest thing she remembered was the soft feel and the sweet smell of her grandmother's warm little lap, and the prickly ruffles she had leaned her infant head against. And the very season, the cool, dry, brown fall, reminded her, for it had been at about this time each year that her grandmother had come south to stay with them until spring. She had come south, that is, a hundred and fifty miles, from south of the center of Texas to the edge of the Gulf of Mexico. But no lady wintered in the south with more style; she came in her pretty hat and her frilly dress, her handsome white hair piled high, the gold hoops swinging from her pierced ears, supervising, with her little lace-gloved hands with their two wedding rings, the arrival of the trunks and the boxes and the suitcases— in one of which would be something exciting for Margaret.

Her mother always saw to it that she went to school scrubbed and starchy and with all her schoolbooks in her satchel; but it was her grandmother who put a ribbon in her hair. Her mother made sure that she ate her vegetables and did her reading by a good light, but her grandmother saw to it that she had a birthday party. Her mother had told her what to do—and even now her mother, her timid, gentle mother, sometimes lapsed into the habit of authority, and Margaret, with the terrible impatience rising in her, choking her, lapsed into being thirteen again; but her grandmother had been her friend. And her grandmother, her foolish old grandmother who believed that crops should be planted at the new moon and that herring on St. Sylvester's Day assured good luck in the coming year, had had a special advantage as Margaret grew older. Parents became merely old-fashioned and embarrassing; they were like furniture that is getting shabby and out of fashion; they were not smart and modern, but not old and different enough to become quaint, valuable heirlooms to which one could point with pride and say, "Handed down in the family, you know."

There in the big living room they had sat, all the winter evenings of her childhood, her grandmother on one side of the fireplace, doing the family's mending, and having her glass of wine to thicken her blood, and talking in German to her mother, in the middle; and her father on the other side of the fireplace, reading. At the table across the room Margaret and her brothers would sit, doing their homework. And the room had been alight with a warmth and safety and peace that seemed as if they would go on forever. But now, in the harsh morning sunlight, and to her middle-aged eyes, the vast room of her childhood was shrunk to very ordinary proportions; the fire was out, and there were only ashes on the hearth; the actors were gone from the stage, for their cues had sounded elsewhere, and the props were naked in their shabbiness.

That mending, Margaret suddenly thought, was really the only thing her grandmother had ever done that had given her pain. With all her love of prettiness and properness, she never darned anything in matching colors. Margaret spent her schooldays wearing knee-length gray hose with heels, showing a little above the edges of her shoes, darned in green; or blue darned in red. Why was it? she wondered. Was it some gay old peasant tradition, or could her grandmother have been color-blind? She didn't think she had ever complained about it; her grandmother was too good, too loving, too proud of her neat, soft darns to be complained to. Margaret just wore the hose and suffered, convinced that every child in school looked at them and laughed.

Some of the living-room furniture was different now; but the chair her father had sat in was still there by the fireplace, a battered wooden rocker that, even when Margaret was a child, her grandmother thought needed replacing with something better. It had been given him by his students when he had quit teaching school. Margaret had thought her grandmother was quite right; but now, dusting between the rungs, she decided that it was not really much worse than the rest of the furniture; she supposed that his students must have liked him, and that it was quite reasonable that he was fond of the chair and liked to sit in it. It occurred to her that perhaps her grandmother had not been very tactful about it. But she was tired of remembering it all, and she put away her dustcloth and went outside to sit in the sun.

IV

In the milk room, Jim Holmes was turning the cream separator. A gush of frothy white skim milk poured out of the larger faucet, and a small, yellow stream of cream poured from the other. He was glad Margaret was home. Life had seemed so gray and grim, with Anna's mother in bed all the time, and needing a lot of care, while they all waited for death. Margaret was a good girl, he thought; it cheered them all up to have her there. Well, all his children were good children, and he wished he could do all sorts of things for them. And he schemed and planned, as he often did, about how they would work for a few more years, and if they had some good crops, and no bad droughts, maybe they could be quite proud of what they left to their children. But the trouble with that was that Anna was going to have to take it easy; he was still able to do anything, but Anna wasn't as strong as she used to be. Things had been pretty hard for her since her mother had been so low, particularly since her mother had been acting cranky toward her. But the poor old woman didn't mean a thing by it—it was just that her mind wasn't clear anymore. He supposed that she had been a good woman in her way. She was always good to the children. Poor Margaret, he thought, too; it's not a very joyful homecoming for her; I must try to make things more cheerful for her. His pity enveloped them all; he was the one who must care for them all; but in the midst of it, he moved a bucket and landed half a quart of skim milk on the floor, and swore, for he was a quick, irritable man.

His thoughts, wandering, lit on Mrs. Snelling, and a frown crossed his face. Mrs. Snelling was after him about the local dance hall. The last time she had come steaming down the road to the farm in her little gray car to see him, she had leaned forward dramatically and fastened her burning black eyes on his and said, "I tell you, Mr. Holmes, that there's drinking, and dancing, and sinning going on at that place, and something has got to be done about it. And it's not only that you're the justice of the peace, but that you're the only man in this whole community with backbone enough, and religion enough, and respect enough, to stand up and do something about it." She had fastened her black eyes on him hypnotically. He was in an uncomfortable position, for he too was against drinking and dancing and sinning, but he had no plans to do anything about it.

"Mrs. Snelling," he said, "you and I know that drinking and dancing and sinning are wrong, but I don't know as there's any law on the statute books against them. Maybe a case could be made out that the dance hall's disturbing the peace, but there's nobody lives within two miles of it to disturb, and frankly I doubt it'd hold up."

"Mr. Holmes!" Mrs. Snelling almost screamed at him. "This isn't the attitude I would expect from you! You know and I know that the Kingdom of God is not to be won by shilly-shallying around like this!"

"Well," he said, "you have to be sort of thoughtful about proceeding in the name of the Kingdom of God."

He had gotten rid of Mrs. Snelling finally, but somehow he didn't think she was going to leave it at that. Well, he sighed, she was a good Christian woman, he supposed. He took a bucket of skim milk into the kitchen for Anna's cats. Cussed cats, he muttered, out of habit.

V

Moreover, something else was cussed. As he came into the kitchen, Jim said that he was cussed if he could understand why he didn't have a whole pair of socks. Anna turned wearily around and, looking thin and tired and plaintive, said, "Why Jim, you *know* I haven't had time to darn any socks for you, as busy as I am with Mother."

"I know, I know," he said testily. "I'm not blaming you. I'm just cussed if I can understand what happens to socks nowadays."

"Maybe I could darn a few pairs for you, Dad," said Margaret—and as she said it, she wondered if she really could. She hadn't darned any in years; Roger had given up the idea, disillusioned, early in their marriage, and now he threw them away quite cheerfully when they developed holes. But it was not something she could suggest to Dad, for things weren't done that way at home.

As it turned out, she enjoyed darning the socks. It was almost exciting; each gaping hole was a chasm across which she threw a warp (she thought, happily mixing her metaphors), and then back and forth she plied, building the woof. She finished a striped pair, a blue pair, a wine-red pair; just as she had occasionally as a child undertaken some task willingly and enjoyed it because she planned to surprise the grown-ups with how much she had accomplished, so she pleasantly anticipated how Dad would exclaim with surprise when he saw how many she had mended. For he had said apologetically, "Oh, I hate for you to spend your time that way, Mag—this should be your vacation. Well, if you want to darn one pair for me, that would be just dandy."

She picked up a pale gray pair; one was perfect, but the other had a hole in the heel. There was no gray thread except some rather puny cotton, which would take forever to darn with and might rub the foot a little. She contemplated the rosy wine-red wool she still had in her needle and thought that it would do nicely; it was thick and soft. Back and forth she darned, humming a little under her breath. The colors were beautiful together, the rich wine red on the soft pale gray. Suddenly she stopped and looked with a shudder at what she had done; perhaps it was a hereditary taint, which came out remorselessly now and again down through the generations, and there was no escaping it.

VI

"Can I help you with anything?" Margaret asked her mother, coming into the kitchen.

"Well, I was thinking about making a pecan cake.

Would you like that? Well, then, if you wouldn't mind shelling a cup of pecans for me. They're in the big brown bag in the pantry. And here, if you'll just spread out this paper towel to catch the mess. Aren't you chilly without a sweater? You know you always were a little susceptible to colds, Margaret. Oh no, not that cup," she added. "That was your great-grandmother's. It's the only thing of hers I've got, and I'm very particular about it."

"All *right*," said Margaret. "Where's the nutcracker?"

"Oh, you don't want the nutcracker," said her mother. "It squashes them so. You want the little crate hammer. Just one good tap on each end, and the halves come out without breaking."

Margaret sat down moodily at the kitchen table, feeling slightly chilly without a sweater, with the paper towel, and the aluminum measuring cup, and the little crate hammer; and the coil of dark hair at the back of her head silently unlooped itself and slithered down and wound itself into two long braids hanging down her back; and two red darns grew in the heels of her stockings; and her firm, good-natured, grown-up mouth grew soft and unformed, slightly open and sulky.

They worked in silence for a while, and then her mother said suddenly, in a rush, hurrying to get it out before embarrassment overcame her, "You know, Margaret, there's one thing I feel real bad about. Mama being here with us, so low and all, and my being so busy with her and upset by her lots of times, is hard on your father, and sometimes it doesn't seem fair, especially since she never liked him anyway."

Margaret looked up, shocked. "She never *liked* him! What makes you say that?"

"Well, of course she didn't," said her mother mildly. "She had a fit because I married him, in the first place."

"You mean she really *objected*?" breathed Margaret, dumbfounded.

"Let us say," said her mother wryly, "that our marriage never had her blessing."

"What did she have against him?" asked Margaret.

"Just didn't like him," said her mother. "They didn't have anything in common. And then, of course, she probably would have objected to anybody that she hadn't picked out herself. She was always determined to manage me. None of the rest of the children, just me. To this day she talks to me sometimes as if I were thirteen, and sometimes I'm silly enough to go off by myself and shed a tear about it, just as if I *were* thirteen.

"You know," she went on, "your father never had

a chance in his whole married life to enjoy his own fire-side. Mama made up her mind that she was going to spend every winter with us, and she did; and every winter evening we would sit there by the fire, and your father would try to read, and Mama would insist on talking in German to me, knowing he couldn't under-stand and that it must get on his nerves sometimes. And she would pick that one time of the day when we were together to have her nip of wine, just because he was a teetotaler and she knew it made him wince a lit-tle. But she knew he'd made up his mind, that he had his own ways but wasn't going to push them on any-body else, and she just liked to rub her ways in on him.

"Anything he ever did that didn't turn out well, or anytime he ever lost his temper at you children, or any-thing like that, she would sort of bide her time and then take a dig at him, in her rather gentle, ladylike way. And while I was grown up enough so that I went ahead and married him, I wasn't grown up enough so I didn't let her influence me sometimes. If life ever seemed hard with your dad—which sometimes it has, because he's not a patient man—you can bet I could get plenty of sympathy from Mama. Well," she concluded, "when it comes to the big things, your father's been awfully good and awfully understanding, and some-times I think I haven't appreciated him enough, and maybe his children haven't either."

"I-I don't know," said Margaret. "Maybe we haven't."

They heard his footsteps outside, and both of them wiped their eyes hastily and turned to their work.

"It beats me," he said irritably, "why nobody can ever remember that I need *three* milk strainers laid out in the milk room every morning."

"If you didn't leave a couple in the barn," said Anna shortly, "there'd be a better chance of three getting washed and sterilized for each milking."

VII

On Tuesday afternoon Mrs. Birdie Baxter and her mother, Mrs. Doleman, came to call. Mrs. Doleman was eighty-nine, and she was very deaf. But she came with a smile of triumph on her long, waxlike, cultivated, palsied old face, for all these years she, who was three years younger than Mrs. Heldt, had had to be shouted at and read to, while Mrs. Heldt had been able to hear and to do fancywork; but now Mrs. Heldt was down and not likely to get up again. Mrs. Doleman was a lady, but her daughter Birdie was not; she was a tomboy grown middle-aged; her voice was a coarse shout, grown raucous from years of yelling at her mother. She fidgeted with perpetual impatience, and her wry, humorous face twitched.

"Hello, Miz Holmes!" shouted Birdie, as she

yanked her mother up the front steps. "We just thought we'd come by to see how Miz Heldt is and say hello to Margaret—my soul, Margaret, it's years since I laid eyes on you—hello, Mr. Holmes, d'you think we're going to get some rain?" But Birdie's mother interrupted Birdie's clatter; she spoke as one who broke a silence—which she did, for she could no longer hear Birdie's shouts, only her screams. Her voice was low and emphatic; it cut through Birdie's shrill cry as the soft resonance of an organ might drown out the screeches of little children.

"How do you do, Mrs. Holmes," she said, with genteel ceremony. "And dear Mr. Holmes. And dear Margaret."

"How're you, Mrs. Doleman," shouted Mr. Holmes at her. "I hope you've been well lately?"

"I beg your pardon?" said Mrs. Doleman in her quiet, resonant voice.

"I HOPE YOU'VE BEEN WELL LATELY?"

"I am but poorly, Mr. Holmes, thank you kindly," said Mrs. Doleman, as Birdie deposited her on the sofa and propped her cane up beside her. They pulled their chairs close.

"I suppose your mother's about the same?" yelled Birdie, leaning across her mother toward Anna. "Could we step in and say hello to her? She's asleep? MIZ HELDT'S ASLEEP, MAMA."

"You know how it is," said Anna. "Not much

change, but I suppose she gets a little weaker all the time. And her mind wanders so, of course; sometimes she doesn't really know much about what's going on, although other times she surprises me and acts real natural for a while."

"Well, at her age you can't expect much," said Birdie. "Really, she's been awfully spry and alert all these years. Not like Mama," she shouted, and she leaned over carelessly and tucked in the little comb that was threatening to fall out of her mother's back hair. "Poor thing, she's been getting more and more childish for years now till I swear, sometimes I don't know what I'm going to do with her."

Mrs. Doleman sat lost in her own thoughts, tall, straight, and dignified, with her faint, triumphant smile on her mummylike face. "Mr. Holmes," she said suddenly, rousing herself, her low, emphatic voice cutting through Birdie's shout, falling in the faintly tragic minor cadence of an Episcopalian priest's. She turned to him, laying her trembling hand portentously on his arm. "Mr. Holmes, the world is in its last days."

"NO DOUBT ABOUT IT, MRS. DOLEMAN, NO DOUBT ABOUT IT," bellowed Mr. Holmes. Mrs. Doleman withdrew her hand and sat back in her chair, mollified.

"Well, I tell you one thing, Anna Holmes," shouted Birdie. "You're having a pretty hard time with your mother down so bad and all, but you ought to thank your stars she hasn't been on your hands all these years, the way Mama has me. I tell you, a person can love her mother as much as anybody, but sometimes I think—"

The quiet, authoritative voice of Mrs. Doleman broke in. "Don't twitch, Birdie," she said.

"Well, it *is* hard," said Anna. "Their ways just aren't ours, I suppose."

Mrs. Doleman's trembling hand sought Mr. Holmes's arm again, fixing him. "Mr. Holmes," she said, "it is five years ago that I last saw the beach at Corpus Christi. And what I saw there with these old eyes of mine was young men and women, and some not so young, flinging themselves around on that beach with next to nothing on, lolling around and laying around, and preening themselves and exposing themselves for all to see. It is a terrible thing, Mr. Holmes, to court the wrath of the Lord! Many a time I have gone down on these old knees of mine and wrestled with the Lord, begging Him and imploring Him to spare Corpus Christi the fate of Sodom and Gomorrah!"

Birdie slapped one leg across the other, flung one arm over the back of her chair, and gave her girdle a hitch and her face a twitch. "And I tell Mama," she yelled, "that she better do her praying standing up after this. Last time she was on her knees about Corpus Christi, I like to never got her up again."

"I trust," said Mrs. Doleman suddenly, turning to

Anna, "that Mrs. Heldt has the comfort of her religion?" There was a slight emphasis on the *her,* for it was not Mrs. Doleman's religion.

"Well, I guess so," said Anna weakly; religion was not her mother's strong point.

"I beg your pardon?" inquired Mrs. Doleman.

"OH YES, YES SHE DOES!" shouted Mr. Holmes.

Mrs. Doleman sat back in her chair, satisfied. She had always suspected Mrs. Heldt of being a light woman, but perhaps she was repenting in the end.

"Well, I'd better be getting along home and cooking up a mess of pablum or something for Mama's dinner. She gets cranky as heck if her meals are late," shouted Birdie. "MAMA"—her voice welled to a scream as she stood up and gave her mother an upward haul—"IT'S GETTING LATE, AND WE'D BETTER BE GOING ALONG!"

VIII

Wednesday morning Anna and Margaret lingered over their coffee at the breakfast table after Jim had gone outside to his work.

"Margaret," said her mother heavily, "there's something I want to talk to you about. You know that Mother's likely to pass away any day now, and a person just can't help but think ahead about some of the problems. I know people don't seem to go in much for mourning anymore, but you know my best coat is that rose-colored one, and I just don't see how I can wear that to my own mother's funeral, do you? But you know I never wear anything black. I don't suppose you've got anything black to lend me, either."

Margaret shook her head dumbly. She knew why her mother hadn't anything black; she looked like a little old crone in black, and so did Margaret. It was their complexions; they were sallow.

"If I weren't so *old*," her mother said plaintively, looking like a sad little child. "If I were only fifty, or something, a rose-colored coat wouldn't seem so bad. But I'm seventy-three, and it'd look awfully bad, I'm afraid."

Margaret regarded the problem with distaste. She was prepared to face Death, for others and for herself, and give it its due, to grieve and expect no comfort. She was prepared to be remorselessly realistic about Death, to face without a qualm the thrifty eventual return of them all to the universal compost heap—even her own husband and children, although at the moment they hardly seemed alive enough to matter, for she was back among the real people, and these figures who had come into her later life seemed only faintly outlined, lightly sketched, and far away. In short, she felt very mature about Death; but it shocked her profoundly to be asked to consider what one should wear to one's mother's funeral. And yet she could not turn away from the problem; for as she sat there looking at her mother, and saw how worn and tired and worried and frail she looked, she felt that she loved her. And besides, she could not help but see that if she herself were not, in all probability, going to be safely far away when the event occurred, so that Death would be only an abstraction named in a telegram, the same problem might cross her mind—for the only coat she had with her was a striking Chinese red. And if rose were unsuitable at seventy-three, what could one say for Chinese red at thirty-seven? Never mind, she thought hastily; Dr. Thompson keeps saying she's awfully strong for her age, and surely nothing will happen before next Friday when my plane leaves.

The female part of her mind, having nosed in the door, sniffed delicately around the edges of the problem, sank its teeth in it experimentally here and there, decided that it was, after all, only a rather special case of the general question of what to wear, and settled down on the hearthrug with it.

"I don't suppose you've got anything navy blue, or maybe gray?" she asked.

Her mother shook her head. They made her look sallow, too. "I've got the light blue, and it's still perfectly good, but I got tired of it. But it's just as light colored, really, as the rose. I can't see as it would be much better."

"Maybe you could get it dyed," Margaret said. "If the material is still good, it ought to dye black beautifully, and since you're tired of it anyway, it wouldn't much matter. Later you could just wear it to work in the garden in chilly weather, or something like that."

"You know, I could do that," her mother said. "You know," she said, and her voice sounded stronger, "I *could*. Let's not explain it to your father," she added hastily. "There's some things men are funny about."

IX

Coming in from the backyard, Jim shouted, "Anna, I'm fixing to go down to the post office and get the mail. Is there anything you want me to do downtown?"

"Yes," said Anna, coming into the kitchen. "I've got something in that bag on the table by the side door I want you to leave by the cleaner's. It's something for Mr. Harper to dye, and I've got all the instructions inside, so you don't have to do a thing but leave it."

Going out the side door on his way to the driveway, Jim looked out across the land to the east. Suddenly he stopped; coming at a fast clip down the road that led to the farm was a little gray car, looking, the thought went through his head, like a horseman of the Apocalypse. He muttered to himself hastily and ritualistically, as another man might cross himself, "She's a good Christian woman," and he headed for the backyard, pausing to pick up a stout mesquite limb from the woodpile in case he met a rattlesnake, although it was not rattlesnake season. He struck out at a quick pace across the western fields, the idiotic, eager black-and-white dog following joyfully at his heels, and the old yellow tomcat following indifferently, at a leisurely distance, as if by coincidence.

Jim Holmes was seventy-five, and he was a short, stocky man, but he was strong and quick, and he was a good walker. By the time Mrs. Snelling had turned in at the farm, gotten out of her car and up the front walk, greeted Mrs. Holmes and Margaret, inquired after Mrs. Heldt, and asked for Mr. Holmes, he was only a speck on the western boundaries of the farm, halfway to the mirage at the horizon. No road led there, no shout could reach that far, and between him and Mrs. Snelling lay a hundred acres of freshly plowed furrows, two Jersey bulls, and three electric fences. Mrs. Snelling stood in the west yard of the house, between the hibiscus bushes and the fig tree, and gazed yearningly across the fields, and her enormous black eyes were burning and tragic.

X

Later, when Jim did go downtown with the coat for Mr. Harper, Margaret went along. In front of the post office, they ran into old Dr. Mercer.

"You remember Dr. Mercer, don't you?" said Jim, and Margaret said of course she did. She had known him distantly all her life. She knew vaguely that he had been, at a time before she could really quite remember, their family doctor, as well as the family doctor for everybody else within twenty-five or fifty miles. Eventually other doctors had appeared, and Dr. Mercer, not so young now, had restricted his practice to a smaller radius. But her parents had always spoken of him rather affectionately, and now, after fifty years of mild acquaintance, her father and Dr. Mercer, two little white-haired men, threw their arms around each other's shoulders lovingly.

She even knew what Dr. Mercer's tragedy was. He had had pneumonia seven times in his life, and it had become his special enemy. And as befits a special enemy, he had studied it and learned its ways. After the younger doctors had taken over a lot of the croup and measles and baby delivering, he had become a sort of specialist in pneumonia. When a doctor felt uneasy about a patient, and thought of pneumonia, he immediately called in Dr. Mercer; and Dr. Mercer came and sat by the patient's bed awhile and studied him intently, and listened to his chest, and looked at the color of his fingernails, and after a while he might say that they'd better get him to the hospital. "I'm not sure he's got pneumonia," he would say sometimes. "But I think he's going to have it by tomorrow. I can't tell you why I think so, but I can sort of smell it in the air." And he was always right. "Oh, I know pneumonia," he would say cheerfully, when people mentioned this talent of his. "It's one thing in this world I really know. I've had it seven times, and it'll get me in the end. It's my old enemy, and I'm wise in its ways."

But Dr. Mercer was almost eighty now, and pneumonia hadn't gotten him. Penicillin had been discovered, and his diagnostic nose wasn't needed anymore, for they cured pneumonia without bothering to diagnose it first. Dr. Mercer went on cheerfully enough, but he was never quite the same; he became just an old-fashioned, behind-the-times country doctor, and the young never asked his opinion again.

Of course she remembered him, Margaret said, and she shook his hand warmly. "You ought to," Jim remarked. "You know, Margaret, this is the doctor that brought you into the world."

Margaret looked at Dr. Mercer with intense interest. She had never heard that; nobody had ever mentioned who had officiated at her birth, nor had she thought to wonder about it; but suddenly she felt a bond with this amiable little white-haired man, who had been her first, her oldest acquaintance in all the world, a bond so strong that she wondered that she had never noticed its pull before.

"I certainly did," Dr. Mercer said jovially. "She looks like her mother now, and she looked like her the day she was born."

"For that matter, Margaret," said Jim, "he delivered your brothers, too."

"I certainly did," said Dr. Mercer. "And I never saw a finer bunch of babies than the Holmes family had." He put a hand confidentially on Margaret's arm. "One thing I want to tell you right now. You all may have thought, sometimes when you were growing up, that your dad was a little hard-hearted, but I just wish each of you could have seen his face the day you were born." And he sprang back and smiled at them, as if he had created them both.

At lunch, Margaret said, "Well, I got reacquainted with the doctor who delivered me, Mom."

"*What* are you talking about?" asked Anna.

"We saw Dr. Mercer downtown," explained Margaret.

"Dr. Mercer didn't deliver you," said Anna.

"Why, sure he did," said Jim, startled. "Margaret and the boys too, didn't he?"

"Jim, I'll swear, I don't know what you're thinking about," said Anna. "Don't you remember that when Joe was born I went home to Mother's, and when James was born Dr. Mercer was away at the First World War, and when Margaret was born they had that new obstetrician in Corpus Christi, and Dr. Mercer suggested I have him."

"But," protested Jim helplessly, "he remembered all about it!"

"You give Dr. Mercer a few clues," said Anna shortly, "and he'll remember anything."

XI

Anna didn't generally pay much attention to old Mrs. Doleman, but the question stuck in her mind and came back to her at odd moments: Had her mother the comfort of her religion? Anna wasn't much interested in religion, really; when the children were small and had asked her questions about strange, unexplained things they had heard at Sunday school (But Mama, who was the Holy Ghost? Was he really Jesus' daddy?) she had looked nervous and told them to ask their father, or else she had said stiffly, "There are just some things we aren't meant to know," and hastily escaped to check on her mockingbirds, or to weed her garden. The things that were living and growing, the view from her kitchen window, the sunrises and sunsets, were enough for Anna, and philosophizing made her restless.

It had never occurred to her to want the comfort of any religion at any time so far in her life, and it would probably not cross her mind when she died; but for someone else—for her mother, now that the idea had been put in her mind—she wanted all the comfort there was. Of course, the young Lutheran minister had been to see her mother, a couple of weeks ago; but it was hard to see, really, that it had counted for much, one way or the other. The young Lutheran minister was named Baumgarten, and he was the grandson of an old Pastor Baumgarten who had christened Anna and her brothers and sisters, long ago. But somehow the young Baumgarten didn't belong to the fine old breed of Lutheran ministers, who had plain, stout wives, and ten well-behaved children, and the thin ascetic faces and deep burning eyes of impassioned monks, and ringing, authoritative voices. The young pastor was fresh out of seminary and knew of quite a few more things than had been dreamed of in his grandfather's philosophy. But he spoke only English, and he hadn't worn his cassock the day he had come—perhaps knowing that Jim, although he would certainly be polite, would hardly be able to suppress a Puritan start at the sight of a clerical robe fluttering through his house.

And the minister was so dreadfully young. He had come determined to do his pastoral duty, but he had not known, really, how to go about offering the comfort of her religion to an old lady who was dying. It had been one of her more confused days, and she had thought that he was one of her grandsons, and seemed inclined to think that he was Raymond, the one who always got on her nerves. So although he had tried to ask for the repentance of her sins and to offer her, in exchange, the glories of the life everlasting, it had been uphill work. Finally he had offered up a little prayer and escaped, pressing Anna's and Jim's hands earnestly, with a look of relief on his fresh young face.

So Anna couldn't really see that much had been accomplished. But the trouble was that she had no idea of what her mother required in the way of religion. Her mother had for years had on her living-room wall a motto, with Gothic letters embroidered on pink silk, sprinkled with silver dust, and hanging by a lavender silk tassel, which said *Der Herr ist in die Heimat.* And she had always been a churchgoer; but when Anna thought about it, all that rose before her was a long succession of churchgoing clothes: the summer starched dimities and dotted swisses with flounces and ruffles and little pleats, and the winter lavender or black silks with the delicate lace collars, and the pretty hats, their rosebuds or violets blurred by the encircling veiling, and underneath, her mother's fresh face with the faint touch of powder on the nose, happy with the propriety and sociability of the occasion, lingering on the church lawn with the other ladies in the noontime sun.

She could not possibly have understood those sermons she listened to so dutifully. She hadn't the vocabulary, either in German, which all the sermons used to be preached in, or in English, as they were in later years, with German only every fourth Sunday. Those sermons had been recondite in vocabulary and austere in content; those old ministers had had no tradition of homely metaphor or folksy illustration.

Of course, perhaps understanding sermons didn't really matter, Anna thought vaguely; she had never heard that it was a requirement for entering the Kingdom of Heaven. Still, to Jim the sermon was everything. Modern city churches irritated him with their printed programs with introductory music and introits and doxologies and choirboy choruses and soprano solos and offertories and announcements trailing down them, and lost somewhere in the shuffle the item, *sermon*. What Jim expected in church was a good, solid sermon, with a well-chosen text, properly understood, well presented, well applied—a sermon with a beginning, and a middle, and an end, with some sound reasoning in it and perhaps just a touch of evangelic fire.

When a new minister came, or a visiting minister appeared, Jim went to church eagerly, and listened with urgent concentration. But as the sermon proceeded, he would often begin to glower; and on the way home his movements would be so tense and wrathful, the cloud on his brow so threatening, that Anna and the children would hold their tongues. Finally he would burst out, "That young man may be filled with the spirit of the Lord, but his logic's damned poor!" Sometimes Jim would be reminded of a favorite joke of his—about the ministerial aspirant who, after delivering his first sermon, saw the letters *GPC* emblazoned in light across the evening sky, and knew that his call to the ministry had been confirmed, for he interpreted them to mean "Go preach Christ," unaware that the weary Lord had telegraphed, "Go plow corn." Jim's family would laugh pallidly; they were relieved that the storm had passed, but they had heard the joke before.

Getting back to the problem of her mother, Anna decided to ask Jim about it. Religion was his department in their house. He had a firm, authoritative air about it; he seemed always to know what you were to do about it, and when enough had been done about it and you could dismiss the whole thing from your mind.

After dinner when they were alone together, she

began timidly, "Jim"—the very words came awkwardly to her; she never knew how people could *talk* about such things—"do you think Mama's feeling any lack of religion? Do you think she feels she's, well, uh, *saved*?"

"Don't talk rot," said Jim irritably. "Your mother may have had her faults, but she's always been a good Christian woman." Anna subsided contentedly. Jim knew about these things.

XII

Mrs. Ewing, the practical nurse, had moved to town long after Margaret had left home, and she had never known her. It was important, Margaret realized, that she should take some occasion to be friendly to Mrs. Ewing, for help was hard to find, and besides, any putative stuck-upness in the Holmes daughter come back from the city would, if Margaret read the signs aright, be analyzed around town for some time to come. So Thursday afternoon when Mrs. Ewing came down to the kitchen for a cup of coffee, Margaret lingered to chat with her.

"I hear you have a fine family of boys," Margaret said.

"Well, yes I do," said Mrs. Ewing. "Johnny, that's the youngest one, is still in high school, and J.B.'s working for the Farm Bureau Gin, and Ralph"—she settled back proudly in her chair—"is an airline pilot. He was in the Air Force, you know."

"That must be interesting," said Margaret. "Traveling all the time."

"Yes, he certainly gets around," said Mrs. Ewing. "He's in St. Louis one night, and back in Corpus Christi the next, and that's the way it goes. Lots of people ask me if I don't worry about him, flying all the time like that, but I don't."

"It's wonderful you don't," said Margaret. "Lots of people would, I guess, and it would just make it hard on them."

"It's my religion," explained Mrs. Ewing. "I believe what's going to be's going to be, and that we all have our appointed time, and nothing can change it. Now, it's just the same with your grandma. Lots of people are surprised at her hanging on as long as she has, but I'm not. I tell them she has her appointed time, the same as all of us, and nothing can hurry it."

Margaret wound her long legs uneasily around her chair, and the conversation lapsed.

Mrs. Ewing shifted herself in her seat, cleared her throat in a preparatory way, and folded her arms. Finally she said firmly, "There's something I want to ask you, if you don't mind."

"Oh, of course, go right ahead," said Margaret nervously.

"*Why don't you get a permanent?*" asked Mrs. Ewing in a cold, hard voice.

"Well, I don't know," said Margaret, putting a jittery hand up to her straight dark hair and tucking a hairpin back into the knot at the back of her head. "I just guess I . . . I sort of like to . . ." She trailed off nervously.

"Don't people *get* permanents in the East?" asked Mrs. Ewing.

"Well, not so much—no, not so much as here. Lots of people, really, you'd be surprised how many people there don't . . ." Margaret babbled.

"Well, it certainly is queer, ain't it?" Mrs. Ewing said more genially, and, fondly patting the gray curls that lay, tensely coiled and ready to spring, all over her head, she gathered herself up and started back to the sickroom.

XIII

After Anna had finished the dinner dishes, it occurred to her to wonder where Jim was. He wasn't in the living room reading, as he usually was in the evenings. Stepping into the hall that led to her mother's room, she heard his voice rising and falling in a regular rhythm. Curious, she walked quietly down the hall and peered in the door; and there was Jim, pulled up in the rocking chair close to her mother's bed, his old white head bent over his Bible, reading aloud. He read well; he belonged to a generation that read aloud to each other, without hurry or apology. His voice was not particularly melodious, but it was strong and sure; he read with authority, with the conviction that what he read was good poetry and sound sense; he approved of it.

> *Oh God, thou art my God; early will I seek thee:*
> *My soul thirsteth for thee, my flesh longeth for*
>   *thee*
> *In a dry and thirsty land, where no water is;*
> *To see thy power and thy glory,*
> *So as I have seen thee in the sanctuary.*
> *Because thy lovingkindness is better than life,*
> *My lips shall praise thee.*
> *Thus will I bless thee while I live:*
> *I will lift up my hands in thy name.*

And peering around the door, Anna saw her mother, propped up with an extra pillow behind her back, gazing at Jim with a happy, trusting look in her sunken old eyes, a faint, demure, churchgoing smile on her lips, and with, somehow, in the tilt of her head, an air of decent, prettily hatted decorum.

XIV

It was time for Margaret to go home; her plane left on Friday morning. Her husband and children, whom she had almost forgotten, now rose before her vivid and real, industriously doing all the things they should not do, and failing to do all the things they should do, and needing her badly. Roger would by now have used up all his decent shirts and, neglecting to take them to the laundry, would be wearing frayed cuffs to the office. The children would have either forgotten their lunch money or taken the wrong amount often enough to have arrived at a complete impasse with the school cafeteria, and be sitting, thin and waiflike, on the school steps at noontime. Ragged, gaunt, and vita-minless, Roger and the children would be using the best china, forgetting to put the cat out, leaving all the lights burning, neglecting the potted plants, and catch-ing colds; and it was time for her to hurry home to them and tell them what to do and when to do it.

She went to her grandmother's room to say good-bye. Perching on the side of the bed, she took her grandmother by her thin little shoulders, but her grandmother shrank away from her.

"You better not kiss me, Margaret," she said seri-ously. "I don't know—I seem to be sick all the time these days." She waved feebly at the hospital bed, the bottles of medicine on the bedside table, and Mrs. Ewing, in white, at the foot of the bed. "They talk so much about germs nowadays. We used not to talk about germs."

"I'm not afraid," said Margaret. "It's just something going around, Grandmother, and I guess we'll all get it sooner or later." And she kissed her grandmother's soft, wilted old cheek firmly. She smiled at her and said, "Now you be a good girl while I'm gone"— the old admonition of childhood, which had never been an admonition at all, but only a helpless cry of love. "I will," her grandmother said, and smiled back at her, "and you be a good girl, too."

Mrs. Ewing looked on, chewing her gum attentively, her thumb holding her place in her magazine. She was interested in how people from the East said such good-byes, but a little dissatisfied. She would have thought there'd be more to it than that.

XV

The house seemed so unbearably quiet and empty after Margaret was gone that Anna welcomed the diversion that drew up in front on Friday afternoon. It was an ancient rattletrap of a car, its fenders flopping. Nine or ten Mexicans climbed out and came up the front walk. A cluster of men surrounded a cocky, swaggering young caballero in a stiff new khaki shirt open at the throat, new khaki pants, and a new, pearl-gray ten-gallon hat; and following behind them several giggling women accompanied a girl in a satin dress of a jarring red, a late purple hibiscus bloom in her dark hair, her mouth thick with lipstick, and a red circle painted on each brown cheek. And after them all came an old woman shrouded in her black widow's shawl, her wrinkled beak of a face peering out from under it. Anna went to the door, and the khaki-clad young man said, "Meester 'Olmes? Justice of Peace?" "I'll get him," said Anna.

Jim, summoned in from the field, washed his face and hands and combed his white hair neatly, and then went to the door and invited them in. The bridegroom was named Ramón Torres, and the bride was Rosa María Saldaña. The old woman was her mother, and the rest, the bridegroom explained negligently, with a wave of his hand, were cousins. Jim got out the register, and the bridegroom wrote down his name and his age, 22, with a flourish, and handed it to the bride, who wrote her name and looked at him uncertainly.

"Quantos años," he explained patronizingly, and she wrote 18.

They were from the Johnston ranch, it appeared. They lived in the row of little Mexican houses on the ranch; the men were cattle hands, and the women tended the wood fires in their bare yards, where the pots of pinto beans and tamales cooked, and picked cotton in the summers, and sometimes cleaned and ironed at the ranch house or for people in the town.

Jim pulled up a chair for the mother; probably she was not yet fifty, but her back was bent and her teeth were gone, and the face that peered out from the black shawl looked ancient. He waved the cousins to the background, placed the bride and groom facing him at the fireplace, and began: "Dearly beloved, we are gathered here in the sight of God . . ." There they stood, she gaudy and nervous and shy in her finery, and he with his rakehell cowboy airs, with his new felt hat still on his head; but the firelight shone softly on their smooth oval Indian faces, and their gentle brown eyes were serious.

"Forsaking all others, so long as ye both shall live," read Jim, and he laid his book down. "Now, do you know what that means?" They looked at him dumbly. "That means," said Jim firmly, addressing the bridegroom, "that you're supposed to leave other women alone. And she"—he gestured toward Rosa Maria—"is not supposed to run around with other men. Now you explain that to her, and make real sure you get both sides of it in." The bridegroom looked a little balky, but he spoke to Rosa María in Spanish; she giggled and twisted self-consciously.

"To have and to hold from this day forward, for better for worse, for richer for poorer, in sickness and in health." Jim put the book down. "Now, the point is, you're supposed to stick together and take care of each other. She is supposed to take care of you, and cook for you, and look after you if you're sick; but don't forget that you're supposed to look after her too, and if she's sick don't you expect her to work. Explain it to her." The bridegroom translated, and she nodded. "Sí, sí."

"Now are you sure you understand all of it? Is there anything you would like to go over a little more?" No, they thought they understood. "And can you promise to try to do all that?" Yes, they thought so. "I now pronounce you man and wife," said Jim. Then, throwing his old white head back, he spoke as one who addresses an old friend and peer: "Our Father in Heaven, these are Thy children, and they have come here to do the right thing in Thy sight and in the sight of their fellow men. Bless and grant them love, and happiness, and a decent prosperity and peace in which to live their lives and bring up their children. Amen."

"How much?" asked the bridegroom.

"Two dollars," said Jim.

The bridegroom felt in the stiff new khaki pants, and brought out, carefully, one at a time, two dollar bills. Jim took them, smoothed one out and put it in his wallet, and held out the other to the bridegroom.

"Now you give this to your wife," he said. "From now on, what's yours is hers. She's not to waste your money, but she's to have some of it."

The bridegroom looked somberly at the dollar bill and handed it to the bride, who took it and giggled.

They shook hands solemnly all around, and the wedding party filed out. Some of the spring was gone from the bridegroom's step; as he strode down the front walk, his bride following behind him, he wore the sober look of a family man.

Jim, absently humming to himself, "Tum-*tum*-tee-tum," hurried back to his work outside; clouds were gathering, and a stiff wind was springing up from the east, and it looked like rain.

XVI

It was raining. The steady, dreary beat of the rain on the roof was a comforting sound to the old woman, lying propped up in her bed. There wasn't a drought after all; perhaps everything was all right. The sound of the rain mingled with the sound of Jim's voice, for he was sitting beside her reading.

Thou visitest the earth, and waterest it:
Thou greatly enrichest it
With the river of God, which is full of water:

Thou preparest them corn, when thou hast so
     provided for it.
Thou waterest the ridges thereof abundantly:
Thou settlest the furrows thereof:
Thou makest it soft with showers:
Thou blessest the springing thereof.
Thou crownest the year with thy goodness;
And thy paths drop fatness.
They drop upon the pastures of the wilderness:
And the little hills rejoice on every side.
The pastures are clothed with flocks;
The valleys also are covered over with corn;
They shout for joy, they also sing.

Her mind, wandering from the words, was on weddings. Her door had been open, and some sound, some snatch of words, had echoed down the hall. All she really wanted, she thought, was for Anna to be happy. Her plain-looking, plainspoken, funny, timid Anna was the one of all her children she really loved, but she had never said so; it was the secret she had carefully kept from them all their lives. She reached her hand out to Jim and said, "It's all right with me if you marry Anna." And with her worn old hand, with its two golden wedding rings shining, on Jim's gnarled old farmer's fist, she closed her eyes and died.

Acknowledgments

by Stefan F. Gavell

I am grateful to those who made the publication of these stories possible:

To Helen Perry, who conceived the idea of having one of Mary's short stories published in *Psychiatry* as a memorial.

To Jack Star, the Chicago writer and editor whose enthusiasm for "The Rotifer," for Mary's style of writing, and for her gift of storytelling prompted his exclamation, "She deserves to be published," and propelled his sustained efforts to this end.

To David McCormick of IMG Literary, whose professional judgment and extensive experience led him to conclude that these short stories should be brought to the attention of major publishing houses without further delay.

To Lee Boudreaux, whose discriminating judgment and enthusiasm were the final steps leading to publication of these stories by Random House.

To Ann Gavell, my wife, for her invaluable and unfailing help at various stages leading to publication.

About the Author

MARY LADD GAVELL was born in Cuero, Texas, in 1919. Her father was a Methodist minister and teacher and her mother taught German. She grew up on the family farm in Driscoll, Texas, near Corpus Christi. She graduated from Texas A&M University in 1940.

She taught school for a few years and then went to the University of Texas at Austin, where she received a master's degree in linguistics; her thesis was on early Texas English. In Washington, D.C., she worked as a writer for a federal agency during World War II and after the war for the

Food and Agriculture Organization of the United Nations. She went from FAO to the William Alanson White Psychiatric Foundation to participate in editing the works of the late Harry Stack Sullivan. She later became managing editor of *Psychiatry,* the foundation's quarterly journal.

She married Stefan Gavell, a former Polish Air Force officer who served in the Polish, French, and British air forces during World War II. After graduating from Oxford University, he accepted an appointment with FAO, where he and Mary met.

They had two sons, Stefan Michael Gavell, now executive vice president of the State Street Bank of Boston, and Anthony Christopher Gavell, a CPA and composer of music for films and other media.

After her death from cancer in 1967 at the age of forty-seven, *Psychiatry* wanted to publish one of the short stories she wrote in her spare time, as a memorial to her. "The Rotifer" appeared in the May 1967 issue. Subsequently, this story was included in *The Best American Short Stories* in 1968. John Updike chose "The Rotifer" for *The Best American Short Stories of the Century,* published in 2000.

About the Type

This book was set in Sabon, a typeface designed by the well-known German typographer Jan Tschichold (1902–74). Sabon's design is based on the original letterforms of Claude Garamond and was created specifically to be used for three sources: foundry type for hand composition, Linotype, and Monotype. Tschichold named his typeface for the famous Frankfurt typefounder Jacques Sabon, who died in 1580.